Summer Promise

Summer Promise

ROBIN JONES GUNN

BETHANY HOUSE PUBLISHERS
MINNEAPOLIS, MINNESOTA 55438

Summer Promise
Revised edition 1998
Copyright © 1988, 1998
Robin Jones Gunn

Edited by Janet Kobobel
Cover illustration and design by the Lookout Design Group

Scripture quotations taken from *New American Standard Bible* © 1960, 1977
by the Lockman Foundation.

A Focus on the Family book published by
Bethany House Publishers
A Ministry of Bethany Fellowship International
11300 Hampshire Avenue South
Minneapolis, Minnesota 55438
www.bethanyhouse.com

Printed in the United States of America by
Bethany Press International, Minneapolis, Minnesota 55438

Library of Congress Cataloging-in-Publication Data

Gunn, Robin Jones, 1955–
    Summer promise.
    Summary: A summer in California for Wisconsin farm girl Christy
Miller brings her a new image, a moral dilemma involving the local fast
crowd, an encounter with Christianity, and a vortex of questions about what
is important in life.
    ISBN 1-56179-597-6 (pbk.)
    [1. Christian life—Fiction. 2. Popularity—Fiction. 3. California—
Fiction.] I. Title. Christy Miller Series.
PZ7.G972Su   1988
[Fic]   88-11060
                                                                          CIP

99 00 01 02 03 04 05 / 15 14 13 12 11 10 9 8 7 6 5 4 3 2

To all the Christys in my life.

A summer promise
can last forever—if you give your whole heart.

Contents

CHAPTER ONE

Off to a Bad Start

"I hate you! I hate you!" Christy Miller shouted at her reflection in the closet-door mirror. With a wild "Grrrr," she wadded up her beach towel and heaved it at the mirror, watching it wobble and distort her lanky proportions.

"Christy darling?" came a shrill voice from the hallway. "Are you back from the beach so soon?"

"Yes, Aunt Marti." Christy grabbed a brush and pretended to be untangling her long nutmeg brown hair.

Her aunt, a slim, stylish woman in her forties, opened the guest-room door and looked around. "What was all the commotion, dear? Who were you talking to?"

"Nobody. Just myself." Christy answered calmly, trying to suppress the volcano of fiery emotions boiling within her.

"Why aren't you out on the beach, dear? It's a gorgeous day, and here you sit in your room, talking to yourself!" Aunt Marti dramatically pointed her acrylic fingernail toward the door. "You should be out there enjoying yourself!"

Christy bit her quivering lip and didn't answer.

"This is California! Live a little! We didn't fly you all the way from Wisconsin so you could spend the summer hiding in your room. Get out there and make some friends."

Suddenly, the internal volcano erupted with great force, spewing words with the hot tears. "I tried, all right?" Christy choked. "I tried to get in with some of the beach kids, but they're all a bunch of snobs! I can't stand them! They're rude and mean, and they laughed at me."

Christy covered her face with her hands; the tears oozed through her fingers.

"I had no idea!" Her aunt switched tones and ushered Christy to the edge of the bed. "There, there," she cooed. "Tell me what's bothering you, dear."

It took Christy a few minutes to compose herself before she said calmly, "I don't fit in with the people here. They think I'm a nerd."

"Well, are you?" her aunt challenged.

"Am I what?"

"A nerd."

Christy didn't answer. She stared across the room at her reflection in the mirror.

"Well?" her aunt prodded.

"Look at me, Aunt Martha!" Christy said, jumping up from the bed and standing in front of her. "I'm as white as a frosty cone—sort of shaped like one, too! If that doesn't make me a nerd in Newport Beach, I don't know what does!"

"Really, Christy. A frosty cone?"

"Well, look at me." Christy stretched out her arms to provide a full view of her five-foot-six-inch, 110-pound frame. Her one-piece bathing suit covered her Olive Oyl torso like a bright green Ace bandage.

"Tell me I don't look like a frosty cone."

"You don't look like a frosty cone."

"You're just saying that." Christy plopped on the floor and folded her arms across her stomach.

"Oh, come now, Christy. You might be a bit of a late bloomer, dear, but really, you're a very sweet girl, and you've got a lot of potential."

"Yeah, right. Tell that to the surfers out there. The one who said 'Hey! It's a walking green bean.' "

Her aunt looked confused. "What's that supposed to mean?"

Christy let the tears drip and sniffed loudly. "Don't you see?"

"I see that you got upset over a little remark about a 'green bean.' That doesn't make sense at all."

"They meant *me*, Aunt Marti! No other girl on the beach had on a bathing suit like this ugly one! *I'm* the walking green bean!"

Christy covered her face with her hands and cried until the tears ran down her arms. It was the kind of crying that comes from the pit of the stomach and brings a headache with it. The kind that makes a person snort and gasp, and no matter how idiotic you feel or how hard you try, you can't stop.

"Do calm yourself, will you, dear? It's not as bad as all that. We can certainly buy you a new bathing suit easily enough. And just think. They called you a bean, not a frosty cone. See? They're saying you're thin. That's almost a compliment."

Christy gasped in short spasms, trying to relax. Her aunt took the opportunity to make her point.

"This is exactly the reason I told your mother I wanted you to spend the summer with us. You deserve more than your parents can give you right now, and goodness knows your mother and I didn't have much when we were growing up."

Christy wiped her nose with the back of her hand.

"Here. Use this, will you please?" Marti handed her a tissue. "As I was saying, my goal this summer is to treat you to some of the finer things in life and to teach you, Christina Juliet Miller, how to become your own person."

Christy blinked and tried to suppress a wild belch that had

bubbled up as a result of so much sobbing. Too late. The muffled "Urp" leaked out.

"You're certainly not going to make this easy for me, are you, dear?"

"I'm sorry." Christy felt an uncontrollable urge to laugh. "Are you sure you're ready to transform a belching green bean frosty cone into 'her own person'? Could be kind of dangerous!" Christy broke into laughter. Aunt Marti shook her head and didn't join in.

"We'll start tomorrow, Christina. I'll call and make an appointment for you to have your colors done at nine, and then we'll start shopping for your new wardrobe."

Christy instantly sobered. "I didn't bring much money with me."

"Don't be silly! This is my treat. A few outfits are certainly not going to break me. And one other thing. We really should have your hair cut. Something short and stylish. My hairdresser, Maurice, does marvelous work. By the time we're done with you, you'll look and feel like a new person."

She said it with such finesse, Christy almost believed her. A new wardrobe? A new hairstyle? And what did her aunt mean by "having her colors done"?

"Why don't you shower and dress, dear. Your uncle doesn't know it yet, but he's going to take you to an early dinner and a movie tonight." Aunt Marti swished out the door.

Christy approached the mirror with a new perspective. Twisting her long, nutmeg-brown hair onto the top of her head, she posed this way and that way, trying to imagine how she would look with short hair. She couldn't quite picture the change.

She wished Paula were here. Paula, her best friend back home, always gave her advice when it came to major decisions like this. But then, what did Paula know? She was the one who helped her pick out the dumb green-bean bathing suit!

Christy scrunched up her nose and stuck her face close to the mirror, examining her skin for new blemishes. No new and ugly bumps today. But her cheeks were flushed, and her nose was bright red from crying. Even her eyes showed the effects of her crying spree; they were puffy and bloodshot.

"I have such stupid eyes," she muttered. "They're not blue, and they're not green. They're just sort of nothing—like the rest of me."

"Knock, knock," Uncle Bob called out from Christy's open door.

She immediately released her hair and turned away from the mirror, embarrassed that he had caught her in the midst of such scrutiny.

"Looks like we've got a date tonight for the movies." His merry eyes looked at her from beneath his baseball cap. He must have just come back from golfing, judging by the perspiration stains on his polo shirt. "Anything special you want to see?"

"No."

"Okay. I'll take a look in the paper to see what's playing. Your aunt's not much of a movie fan, so I hope you don't mind that it's just you and me."

"No. That's fine."

"We'll leave in about an hour, okay?"

"Okay."

"By the way," he added, lifting his baseball cap and wiping his forehead, "I haven't told you yet, but I'm glad you came to stay with us this summer." Then he added, "You are my favorite niece, you know."

"I also happen to be your only niece!"

"Minor detail, my child, minor detail," he quipped, politely closing the door.

With a sigh, Christy flopped onto the bed. She didn't feel like showering, and it wouldn't take her that long to change. With an hour to kill, she decided to write to Paula.

Christy liked to write—especially when she had a lot on her mind. She would get everything out on paper, and then when she reread it, it would be like looking at her own thoughts in a mirror. Usually, things came out clearer on paper than when she tried to say them.

Finding the pad of stationery Paula had given her when she left Wisconsin, Christy set to work.

Dear Paula,

Hi! How's everything back on the farm? The plane trip out here was fun for the first hour, but then it got boring. I didn't see any movie stars at the airport, but I still have your notepad, so I can get some autographs in case I see anybody famous.

Remember when you called last Thursday and I told you I couldn't talk? It was because my parents were giving me a big lecture about my trip out here. They made me promise I wouldn't do anything this summer that I would regret later. Can you believe that?

The funny part is, the only thing I regret is that I ever came here. I hate this place! There's nothing to do, and everybody is so stuck up. It's so boring. At night, all I do is sit around and watch TV.

At least one good thing is going to happen. Tomorrow my aunt is going to take me shopping, and guess what? I'm probably going to get my hair cut! Can you believe it? I'm kind of scared, but I think she's trying to give me a new image or something.

Well, I've got to go. I'll tell you how the big makeover turns out. Just think, you might not recognize me when I step off the plane next September. You'd better write to me.

Love,
Christy

CHAPTER TWO

The Makeover

Christy awoke the next morning to the steady rhythm of the ocean waves outside her window. They sounded like a giant taking deep, relaxed breaths as each wave came in and oozed back out. She drew up the window shades and watched a flock of sea gulls circling the sand, scavenging breakfast. Their white bodies flashed bright and clean against the pure blue of the sky.

Opening her window to breathe in the fresh sea air, Christy found herself entranced by the ocean. Foaming waves broke on the shore, erasing the footprints of two early-morning joggers. Everything looked, smelled, and felt fresh and new.

She quickly dressed and greeted Uncle Bob in the kitchen with a cheery "Good morning!" to which he replied, "And a good morning to you, Bright Eyes! Wait till you see what I've got cooking for breakfast."

"Mmm. Smells like waffles."

"And right you are!" Uncle Bob pulled the first steaming waffle from the waffle iron. "Butter and syrup are on the table, and this one's for you. I made my own batter from scratch and, if I must say so myself, it turned out to be a prize winner."

"I'm impressed!" Christy hurried to spread on the butter so that it would melt into all the little squares; then she poured the syrup slowly so that each little square had just the right amount. Carefully cutting the tender waffle into bite-size pieces, she closed her eyes and drew the first forkful to her mouth.

Suddenly, Aunt Marti burst into the kitchen and shrieked, "Christy darling! What do you think you're doing?"

"Eating my breakfast."

"But, sweetheart, don't you realize how many grams of fat are in that one waffle? That certainly isn't a proper breakfast for a young lady who wants her eyes to glow, her skin to gleam, and her hair to shine!"

"I do? I mean, it isn't?" Christy looked to Uncle Bob for support as she held her first bite only inches from her mouth, the syrup dripping onto her fingers. Uncle Bob only smiled.

Bustling around the kitchen, Aunt Marti whirled something in the blender.

"Here you are, dear. This is much better for you, and it has all the vitamins and minerals you need to make the boys notice you."

She presented Christy with a glass foaming with some kind of protein breakfast drink. "Go ahead, honey. Try it!"

Christy put down her fork and picked up the glass. It looked awful. She took a small sip. It tasted awful, too!

"Yuck, Aunt Marti. You expect me to drink this stuff?"

"Yes! Drink it all, dear. And I've got something else for you here." She pulled from the refrigerator a sectioned grapefruit half, sitting on a glass plate with a white doily underneath it. With an air of satisfaction, Marti presented it to Christy.

"There!" she announced. "Isn't it marvelous? The perfect breakfast! Now hurry and finish while I put on my shoes. We've only got 20 minutes before your draping appointment." Then out of the kitchen and down the hall pranced Aunt Marti.

Christy looked at her waffle and then at her grapefruit. She turned to Uncle Bob, who was suppressing a huge laugh.

"So," he teased, "vitamins and minerals, huh?"

"It's not funny!" Christy returned, trying not to laugh herself.

"I don't know. Sounds like a pretty good breakfast to me."

"Then you drink it!" she said, pushing the glass toward him.

"Not me! Your aunt tried to reform my diet once. Once was enough!"

Christy looked at the protein drink, then at the waffle. Quickly, she stuffed two big bites of waffle into her mouth. "You won't tell on me, will you?" she garbled.

"Your secret is safe with me." Uncle Bob winked, pulling another waffle off the iron. "She really means well, you know."

"I know," Christy said with a sigh. "Uncle Bob? Do you think I should get my hair cut?"

He joined her at the table, studying her face and hair like a photographer looking for just the right angle. "Guess I'm not the best person to ask," he said after some time. "I've always liked your hair the way it is. Your aunt is the one who knows all about hairstyles. Why don't you ask her?"

"That's just it. She's the one who thought I should get my hair cut today, and I'm not real sure about it."

"Well," said Uncle Bob, slicing his waffle, "the only advice I can give you is, 'To thine own self be true.' "

"To my own what?"

" 'To thine own self be true.' It's a quote from Shakespeare. It means always do what you want to do, and don't try to please everybody else. Follow your own instincts. That's been my philosophy for years and probably part of the reason I did so well in real estate. I just followed my instincts, and to my own self I've always been true."

Aunt Marti entered the kitchen dressed in a classy black and white pantsuit that showed off her slim figure. Christy discreetly carried her dishes to the sink and quietly poured the protein drink down the disposal before her aunt noticed.

"I hope you also told Christy that much of your success can be attributed to that wonderful secretary you worked with in your first real estate office." She put her arms around his neck and kissed him on the cheek, leaving a smudge of fuchsia lipstick.

"You know," she went on, "that sweet young secretary you ended up marrying."

They exchanged a smile and a quick kiss.

"See what I mean, Christy?" Uncle Bob pointed out. "It always pays to follow your own inner voice."

"Well, my inner voice says we need to get going!" exclaimed Aunt Marti. She gave Christy a quick glance.

"Is that what you're going to wear, dear? Well, no matter. We don't have time to change. Let's get going."

Christy looked down at her long floral-print skirt and the pink tunic top that hung almost to her knees. It was one of the nicest outfits she had brought with her, and she liked it. Aunt Marti's comment made her feel so out of style. Depression surged inside her like a wave, but she didn't have time for it to overwhelm her as it had yesterday. Aunt Marti was already pulling her silver Mercedes convertible out of the garage.

"Better get going," Bob told Christy. "When your aunt goes into warp drive like this, there's no stopping her."

Uncle Bob was right; with Aunt Marti steering Christy along, the day zoomed by. In the first hour and a half, a striking middle-aged woman "draped" Christy with a variety of colored fabrics to determine which colors were hers and which weren't. She selected a group of paint chips and fabric squares and prepared them in a small packet for Christy to carry with her while shopping.

"These are your colors," the specialist told her. "Don't ever wear a color that's not in your packet."

The bright green of her bathing suit was not in the packet. The light pink of the top she had on was not in the packet. She had never realized what a fashion degenerate she was.

As Aunt Marti and Christy paraded in and out of the fancy department stores, Christy could barely keep up. When it came to shopping, Aunt Marti was in "warp drive." Nothing could slow her down, and nothing was out of her price range.

At noon they stopped for a salad at Bob Burns Restaurant, which Marti said was the only place with atmosphere in all of Fashion Island. Christy thought the place was too dark and quiet to be inviting, but she meekly followed her aunt to a booth. Dropping onto the thick cushion, Christy pushed the bags against the wall.

"I'm afraid we're making rather slow progress, dearie." Aunt Marti squeezed her lemon slice into her iced tea. "Aren't you enjoying this? You seem awfully reluctant to try on anything. Why, you haven't tried on a single bathing suit yet! What do you think the problem is, Christy?"

Christy ran her fingers through the ends of her hair and decided to be honest with her aunt. After all, Uncle Bob had told her to be true to herself.

"I just don't know if I like all the same things that you like. I mean, those two shirts and the pair of sandals we bought are pretty basic, but I don't know if I'm ready for some of those other outfits you were showing me. Plus, I don't know, I just feel weird having you pay for everything. I've never been shopping like this before."

The waitress arrived with their salads and asked Christy if she would care for fresh ground pepper on hers.

Christy stared at her blankly for a moment and then said, "No, I don't think so." She had never been asked that before.

The waitress didn't seem to notice Christy's inexperience; she was already offering to twist the large pepper mill over Aunt Marti's salad.

"Listen," Marti continued, waving the waitress away with a swish of her hand. "I already told you; today is my treat. Now, please don't spoil all my fun! Let's start buying things!"

Christy nodded and pushed her cherry tomato to the side of her plate. "Okay. I'll try to loosen up."

"That brings me to another subject, Christy. You must work at being more outgoing if you want to make any friends with the beach kids. Take control of your destiny, darling! Plan your goals and then go after them. Force yourself to be the one in control. Make the first move! Be aggressive! It's the only way you're going to make it."

"I don't know. That's not really me."

"Then make it you. Set your sights high and tell yourself that anything you want is yours."

Christy finished her salad and hungrily eyed the dessert tray the waitress held before them. "I'll have that chocolate thing there." She pointed to a chocolate torte. "As long as it doesn't have nuts in it."

"Christy!" exclaimed Aunt Marti.

Before Marti could scold her, Christy echoed, "You just said anything I want today is mine, and I want this piece of cake!"

Aunt Marti laughed in a light, happy way that cut through her sophistication, exposing her as the simple hometown girl she once was.

"Okay, you win. Nothing for me, thanks," she told the waitress. "Enjoy your decadent fat grams in a hurry so we can go do some serious shopping."

In the dressing room of the next store, Christy had tried on a dozen bathing suits when Aunt Marti brought in one she seemed to be thrilled about.

"This is marvelous!" she gushed with renewed excitement. "It's not too skimpy like the red one, and yet it's still quite fashionable. Trust me, dear. It will look absolutely stunning on you."

The suit, a black one-piece, had thin straps that crisscrossed in the back. It was definitely not the kind of suit Christy would have chosen for herself, but she was eager to try it on and to hear Aunt Marti's reaction.

Aunt Marti had a reaction all right! "Oh, Christy! Didn't I tell you? It's perfect on you. Simply perfect! Come on, step out of that dressing room and look at yourself in this full-length mirror."

As Christy shyly emerged, Aunt Marti called over her shoulder to the dressing-room attendant, "See my niece in this bathing suit. Doesn't she look marvelous?"

How embarrassing! Christy looked in the mirror and caught the reflection of the attendant smiling and politely nodding her head.

"Should I get it?" Christy asked, staring at the $120 price tag.

"Of course!" Aunt Marti chirped. "Now let's see what else we can find. They have a marvelous selection here."

A half hour later, Christy watched the cashier add up her new wardrobe. Besides the suit, she had three pairs of jeans, six shirts, two dresses, a sweatshirt, a jeans skirt, and four pairs of shorts.

"The total comes to $887.58," said the cashier with a smile.

Aunt Marti whipped out a credit card and asked, "Can you add these on as well?" She handed the cashier a pair of bright yellow earrings.

"They'll go perfect with the sundress, don't you think, Christy?"

Christy was still gasping at the total of the bill. Her mother made most of her clothes, and when they did go shopping, it was traumatic to spend more than $40 at one time. But she was with

Aunt Marti now, and this was Aunt Marti's way of doing things. So she responded with, "Sure. They're great!"

Passing the cosmetic counter on the way out, Marti exclaimed, "Oh good! I'm glad we came this way. I'm almost out of my fragrance."

She asked the clerk for the largest size of "Private Collection" and then said partly to the clerk and partly to Christy, "Say, I've got an idea! Let's have your makeup done while we're here."

The clerk responded graciously, and before Christy knew it, she was perched on a high stool before a mirror with lights tilted toward her. The cosmetic specialist gently smoothed a cotton ball over Christy's cheeks and down her nose, explaining the proper procedure for cleansing facial pores.

This must be a dream, Christy thought as the cosmetician smoothed Autumn Haze shadow across each eyelid. A soft pencil traced the inside ridges of her lids and was gently dabbed to perfection at the outside corners. The brush across her cheeks felt like velvet, and as she pursed her lips, she thought how the lipstick smelled like strawberries.

"There," announced the cosmetician. "Have a look at yourself. What do you think?"

Christy opened her eyes slowly.

"Is that me?" she said in a small voice.

It was her, but it wasn't. She looked older, more mature. And her eyes! She never noticed before, but her eyes really were kind of pretty.

"Her eyes are the perfect shape," the cosmetician said to Marti. "She can do about anything with them colorwise because they're such an unusual shade of blue-green."

"Really?" Christy said, looking at her eyes more closely in the mirror.

"Yes," the cosmetician assured her, tilting her chin up to look at her more closely. "I know models who would kill to have eyes like yours."

Christy couldn't believe it. Little bubbles of excitement burst inside, making her feel lovely and almost as if she had done something she shouldn't have. At home she was only allowed to wear lip gloss. But this—this was wonderful!

"You've done a marvelous job," Aunt Marti praised the cosmetician. "We'll take one of everything you used."

"Aunt Marti!" Christy gasped. "Are you sure?"

"Why yes, dear, and please don't make such a scene! We'd also like your complete line of sunscreen products."

Christy couldn't believe all this was happening to her. "Thank you!"

"You're very welcome, my dear." Aunt Marti handed her the bulging bag of cosmetics. "Now we have one more stop to make, if you're at all interested."

"What's that?" Christy asked, catching her reflection in a shiny display as they passed.

"Why, Maurice's Hair Salon, of course."

Christy flashed a smile at her cunning aunt. "I guess it's now or never!"

CHAPTER THREE

The Dream

At 4:30 they arrived home and found Uncle Bob in the den, sitting in front of his laptop with soft jazz music playing in the background.

"Ta-daaa!" Aunt Marti announced dramatically.

Bob turned around and for a moment looked shocked. Then his dry smile returned.

"Well, now!" he said. "I didn't realize you were bringing a movie star home for dinner! I would have worn something more presentable."

"What do you think?" Christy turned all the way around. "Do you like it? I mean, my hair? Do you like it short like this?"

It was short all right! The front layers hit just below her ears. Maurice had styled the layers around her face and cut thin, wispy bangs. At the salon Christy had moaned that she felt like a pampered poodle, but Maurice overheard and Marti scolded her severely. He seemed offended that anyone should question one of his creations. All the stylists then came over and made gushy comments about how ravishing she looked.

Christy wasn't convinced. She wondered what Paula would think. But since Paula was several thousand miles away, Christy was anxious to hear what Uncle Bob had to say. She knew he would be honest with her.

"You sure surprised me, missy! If you didn't have on the same clothes as the girl who left here this morning, I wouldn't have known it was you. You've become quite a young lady."

Christy sighed in relief. "The guy at the salon showed me how to put this spritz stuff on my hair, and I got two bottles of it. I also got a curling iron, and he showed me how to use that, too. But that's not all I got today! Wait till you see what's in all these bags. I've never been on a shopping trip like this before!"

Excitedly, she opened all the shopping bags to display her new belongings. Soon the couch was covered with clothes, shoes, accessories, and her complete makeup assortment.

"Can you believe this?" Christy asked and giggled. "I wish I could wear it all at once."

Aunt Marti looked quite pleased with herself. "This is just what she needed," she whispered to Bob. "Some new clothes and things to make her feel good about herself. I told you she would snap out of her little slump."

"You were right," Christy squealed. "These earrings go great with this outfit! I can't wait to wear it!"

"Then how about putting it on now, and I'll take my two favorite women out for a celebration dinner," Uncle Bob offered.

"Actually, Bob," Marti said in her take-charge tone of voice, "I've got my women's group meeting tonight, so you and Christy go ahead. Why don't you take her to the Crab Cooker?"

"Okay," Bob agreed. "Sounds good to me. What do you think, Christy?"

She had already scooped up her new clothes and called as she dashed up the stairs, "I'll be ready in five minutes." Amazingly enough, she was.

But when she came downstairs, she saw that Uncle Bob was

on the phone. While she waited for him, Christy noticed that he had changed into a clean shirt and combed his thick, brown hair. A handsome man, he looked much younger than his 51 years. His skin, leathered by too many afternoons on the golf course, had settled into creases around his eyes that deepened when he smiled. His voice, smooth and low, contributed to his easygoing manner, which contrasted so sharply with Aunt Marti's accelerated approach to life.

When Uncle Bob finished his phone conversation, Christy made her entrance into the living room.

Uncle Bob gave a low whistle and offered his arm. "May I have the honor of escorting you to the car, m'lady?"

Christy laughed. "Why certainly, your handsomeness."

As they walked out the door, Aunt Marti called, "Have a marvelous time, you two!"

They arrived at the Crab Cooker to discover they had a half-hour wait before they could be seated. Ordering shrimp cocktails from the walk-up window, they moved through the crowd to a long wooden bench.

"Nice breeze tonight," observed Uncle Bob.

"Smells kind of fishy," said Christy.

"That's because Newport Pier is right down that street." Uncle Bob indicated the basic direction with his plastic spoon. "That's where all the boats bring in their daily catch."

"Wow!" Christy exclaimed. "Look at that car!"

"You mean the Rolls Royce?"

"Yeah!" Then lowering her voice: "Do you think movie stars are in it?"

"Not likely."

"I've never seen a car like that, except on TV."

Christy rose from the bench and tossed her plastic cocktail cup into the trash can. As she did, a convertible sports car roared past her into the parking lot.

"Now that's my kind of car," Bob said when she returned to the bench. "TR6, wire wheels, overdrive. I'd guess that's a '68."

"Oh," Christy responded. Now it was her turn to be unimpressed by a car. However, she considered the college-age guys who were getting out of the car worth noticing. She studied them as they walked toward the restaurant and decided they represented everything she liked about California. Tanned and wearing shorts and T-shirts with surf logos, they stood nonchalantly a few feet away, looking very cool.

For a moment Christy thought they were studying her. She must be imagining it. But then Uncle Bob confirmed her suspicions.

"Those guys are sure checking you out."

"No they're not!" Christy nervously tucked her newly styled hair behind her ear.

"Sure they are. Must be the new outfit and hairdo. Do you want me to ask them to join us for dinner?" he teased.

Christy turned her back to the two guys, who were definitely looking in her direction. "Stop it!" she whispered. "I can't believe you said that!"

"My, my. Your cheeks look awfully red for someone who wasn't even in the sun today."

Just then the hostess called out, "Bob, party of two, please."

"Guess we only got a table for two," Uncle Bob said. "Your boyfriends will have to wait till next time around!"

Christy turned her head away as they walked past the guys. She watched as Uncle Bob smiled and gave them a nod.

Through clenched teeth, she threatened her uncle, "I'm going to kill you!"

After ordering, it took about 20 minutes for the food to arrive.

"Thank God," Bob pronounced when it did come. "I'm starving."

His comment prompted Christy to ask something that had bothered her for a while. "Do you and Aunt Marti believe in God?"

Uncle Bob paused for a moment and then explained, "I guess we feel religion is something personal. Something internal based on what you believe. It's not something you publicize."

"Do you ever go to church?"

"Sure, sometimes. But I've always felt that since God is all around and part of everything, you can worship Him wherever you are. You don't have to go to a church to do that."

As long as she could remember, Christy had gone to church. All her family and friends back home in Wisconsin went to church. As a matter of fact, that's where she had met Paula—in the kindergarten Sunday-school class—and they had been best friends ever since. She had never known anybody who said they believed in God but didn't go to church.

"So," Uncle Bob said, taking a deep breath, "sounded like you and Martha had quite a day shopping. How do you feel about your new look?"

Skewering a plump shrimp, Christy thought for a moment. She liked feeling grown-up and stylish, and secretly she had loved the attention from the two guys out front. Feeling mysterious and attractive pulled her toward a way of life she had never experienced before, but one she had certainly fantasized about.

"You know," she began in her most mature-sounding voice, "I really like it. It's much more the real me, don't you think?"

He smiled one of his wonderful smiles and said, "If you're happy, Christina Juliet Miller, that's all that matters."

That night she washed her face and obediently applied her new astringent and moisturizer before slipping into her nightshirt. The astringent had an antiseptic odor, but the moisturizer smelled like fine perfume as she smoothed it on.

"I even smell rich," she thought, crawling into the four-poster bed and pulling the white eyelet comforter up to her chin.

Uncle Bob's words from the restaurant echoed in her head as she lay in the stillness: "If you're happy, that's all that matters."

Today she had felt happy. Happy in an outside, thrilling sort of way. But the feeling of excitement brought with it a new sense of fear. She had felt this way once last summer on the way back from the Dells. Paula's older brother had let her drive his pickup. She remembered how she hadn't particularly wanted to drive the truck, but both Paula and her cousin had taken their turns, and so Christy couldn't say no when it was hers. She had only gotten up to about 45 while the others laughed and challenged, "Go faster!" She had felt as if her stomach were wadded up into a tight ball that would bounce up into her throat at any minute. Fun? Maybe. Scary? Definitely.

She turned off the light on the oak nightstand and fell asleep, thinking of how she would try to be outgoing tomorrow on the beach—take her destiny into her own hands and all that.

About two in the morning, Christy suddenly sat up in bed, her heart pounding and her nightshirt damp with perspiration. She quickly turned on the light and tried to slow down her frantic breathing.

"Fresh air! I need fresh air!" She couldn't jump out of bed fast enough to open the window. Inhaling the brisk salt air, she felt her mind begin to clear. The roar of the ocean soothed her with its constant curling and uncurling sounds.

"What a horrible nightmare!" she panted, shivering in the night breeze at the memory of her eerie dream.

She had been lying on the beach, when all of a sudden a big wave came up on shore, crashed on top of her, and pulled her out to sea. She had struggled and gasped for air, and when she finally thrust her nose above the waves, in every direction all she could see was water. The land had disappeared. In the distance she saw a rowboat. She tried to swim for it, but long, slimy tentacles of seaweed wrapped around her legs and tried to pull her down. Each seaweedy arm had a voice, and in garbled union they all chanted, "Now-we've-got-you, now-we've-got-you."

At last she reached the boat and frantically grasped the side, ready to pull herself in. Then, for one terrifying moment, she couldn't decide if she should hoist herself into the boat or give in to the seaweed's persuasive pull. She was paralyzed by indecision at the crucial moment. That's when she woke up.

"It was just a dream," she told herself. "A silly, meaningless dream."

She took another deep breath, closed the window, and anxiously paced the floor. "It was just a dream," she repeated.

Then, leaving the light on, Christy dove under the covers and prayed: "Dear heavenly Father, please protect me and keep me safe. Be with my mom and dad and David. Amen."

Praying for her family reminded her of the promise she had made to her parents before she left home. So she added, "And dear God, please help me keep my promise to my parents not to do anything I'll regret. Amen."

Within minutes she fell fast asleep.

CHAPTER FOUR

Surf and Seaweed

Had there been a contest to see who could spend the most time in the bathroom getting ready, Christy would have won first prize the following morning. After nearly an hour and a half of preparations, she opened the door to find Aunt Marti standing in the hall, ready to knock on the guest-room door.

"There you are, honey. We were just wondering how you were coming along. Let's see how you look."

Hoping for some sign of approval, Christy asked, "Well? How do I look?"

"Your hair, dear . . . your hair looks . . . well, I'd say you did a very good job for your first try."

"I think I used too much spritz; my bangs all clumped together."

"Yes, maybe you should use a tad less next time. And perhaps go a bit easier on the eyeliner. But the suit . . . the bathing suit looks marvelous on you with your long legs, dear. You won't always have thighs like that if you take after your mother's side of the family, so watch the starches and keep those legs slim as long as you can."

"Yes, Aunt Martha." Christy's voice showed her irritation at the endless advice.

"Well, you know what they say," Marti quickly added, "nobody can ever be too rich or too thin!"

They both laughed and headed down the stairs.

"Do you have any good books I could take with me to read on the beach?" Christy asked.

"Sure, all kinds, darling. They're on the bookshelf in the den. Take your pick. Are you ready for your breakfast drink?"

Christy shuddered at the thought. "No, I'm not hungry. I'll just take something with me to drink." She pulled a paperback novel from the shelf.

Marti returned from the kitchen with two bottles of flavored mineral water and tucked them into Christy's canvas bag. "There you go! Have a wonderful time, and remember, make an effort to be friendly so you can get to know some of the other young people on the beach."

"Yes, Aunt Martha." Christy quickly ducked into the kitchen, where Uncle Bob was reading the paper.

"Shhhh," she hissed, holding her finger to her lips. Then, opening the refrigerator, she exchanged the mineral water for two cans of Coke.

Uncle Bob winked and went back to reading his paper.

A few thin clouds sailed across the late morning sky as Christy shuffled through the sand. The "young people," as Aunt Marti called them, clustered together down by the jetty where the surfers hung out. The jetty, as Christy had learned from her uncle her first day here, was a long, man-made peninsula of rocks that stuck out into the ocean, creating a calm harbor inlet on one side and the beach's biggest waves on the other.

Christy stopped and watched the morning waves smashing against the jetty. The northern waves first swelled some distance out; then pressing in like a wall, they crashed straight down on the rocks with powerful force.

"Take control of your destiny!" Christy's aunt's words echoed in her head and pounded against her nerves. She lifted her head high and walked straight toward the same group that had laughed at her a few days earlier. With the new haircut and swimsuit, she hoped they would think she was a different girl.

Spreading out her towel, Christy noticed a few of the guys looking in her direction. *So far, so good!* she thought. Then, stretching out on her stomach, she began to read her paperback, playfully wiggling her toes in the sand. She didn't know what would be worse—for them to ignore her again or for someone to come over and actually talk to her.

A few minutes later she cast a shy glance toward the guys to see if she still held their attention. She didn't. They had all fixed their eyes on an unbelievably gorgeous girl coming their way.

Tall and thin, clad in a bikini and sunglasses, she waltzed through the sand. Her blond hair fell to her waist, swishing behind her like the mane of a wild horse. She stopped a few feet away from Christy. Then, as everyone watched, the model beach-beauty settled into the sand and gazed out at the ocean as if posing for a swimsuit ad.

What's she trying to prove? Christy wondered, pretending not to notice her. *Why is she sitting near me? What if the guys come over here to talk to her? What if they talk to me?*

A strong urge to run away swelled up in Christy. But she ignored the way her heart raced and fixed her eyes on her book. Her aunt's voice pounded in her head, "Take control of your destiny! Make the first move! Be aggressive!"

The sweet smell of coconut oil floating from the girl taunted Christy until she looked over and, with great effort, forced out a weak "Hi."

The girl responded eagerly. "That's a good book. Have you

gotten to the part where they get stuck in the taxicab in Hong Kong?"

Christy was startled at her friendliness. "No."

"Then I won't spoil it for you," the girl said with a smile. "But that part in Hong Kong is great, and it's so intriguing."

"Oh," Christy replied, turning to study the girl more carefully. She seemed awfully nice, for a snob.

Then the girl asked, "Have you been in the water yet? Is it very cold?" Christy noticed that she had an unusual accent when she said certain words.

"No," Christy said. Then realizing she wasn't adding much to the conversation, she stammered, "I mean, no I haven't been in yet today, and I didn't go in yesterday, so I don't know if it was cold then, but the day before it was really nice." She hesitated and then asked, "Were you out here yesterday?"

"No, we arrived yesterday. My name is Alissa. What's yours?"

"Christy. Where are you from?"

"We've just come from Boston where my grandmother lives, but this past year we lived in Germany."

"Wow, you're from Germany? Really?" Christy asked in amazement. "My dad has some relatives in Germany. I always wanted to go there."

"We only lived in Germany for the past two years. Before that we lived in Argentina, and before that, Hawaii."

"Wow, that must've been something."

"It has its good points and its bad points. My dad was in the air force. What about you? Do you live here?"

"No, my aunt and uncle do, and I'm staying with them. I live in Wisconsin."

Wisconsin sounded pretty boring compared with Argentina or Hawaii. Alissa didn't scoff, though. Instead, she suggested they go in the water. Christy felt the gaze of the surfers as they started in slowly till they were up to their waists before diving under the foamy waves.

The cool water hit Christy's every pore. *There's no other feeling in the world like this!* Christy thought with exhilaration. To Alissa she said, "I love the ocean, don't you?"

"Definitely!" Alissa replied, bobbing over the top of a mild wave. "You would love the beaches in Hawaii. The water is so warm and clear. You can stay in almost all day it seems. And the waves are perfect for bodysurfing."

"I wish I could bodysurf," Christy lamented. "I'm just too uncoordinated."

"It's all a matter of catching the wave at the right time," Alissa explained. "Like see this one coming? If you wait too long, it will break on you and take you right to the bottom. You have to start kicking and paddling as the wave crests behind you. Then let it carry you to shore, like you're part of it."

The wave behind them rose too big for them to float over, so they held their noses and dove down to the calmer water below. Up they came, treading water as the wave pushed its frothing curve toward the shore.

"Now that would have been a perfect wave to ride," came Alissa's evaluation as she smoothed down her soaking hair. "See, those guys over there caught it. I was told in Hawaii by some surfers that every seventh wave is the one to catch."

They floated over four smaller swells before Alissa pointed out, "See the seventh wave building out there? It should be the best one in this set to ride. You go over it, and I'll try to ride it in. Maybe you can see what I mean about starting to kick before it crests."

With a powerful swell, the wave lifted Christy with the ease of a parent lifting a baby. She watched Alissa gracefully ride the wave all the way to shore. *She makes it look so easy!* Christy thought with a sigh.

The guys down the beach were equally impressed with the graceful Alissa. As she emerged from the water, four of them left their surfboards and jogged over to talk to her.

Christy watched with twinges of jealousy as Alissa, dripping wet, gathered her long hair over her shoulder and wrung the water out. *Oh, to have a body and a personality like Alissa's. She has it made in every way.* Christy both admired and disliked her at the same time.

Absorbed in watching the scene on the shore, Christy didn't notice the huge wave rising behind her. Without warning it broke, pulling her down with its crashing force. She turned a complete somersault under water and, panicking for air, gulped in a choking mouthful of saltwater. The terror of her dream the night before rushed up, causing her to fight something greater than the ocean. Mercilessly, the wave dealt her a final blow, spewing her onto the shore and scraping her elbow in the coarse sand. The wave receded, leaving Christy like a beached seal only a few feet from none other than Alissa and the surfers.

"Oh, no!" she gasped as the group began to laugh. Water dripped from her nose, sand trickled from her ear, her bathing suit straps were all twisted in the back and a long strand of seaweed had wrapped around her ankle. Worst of all, her hair stood straight up in the back and the whole right side lay plastered across her cheek, covering her eye. She blinked, looking to the group for some support, but they all kept laughing. Alissa laughed the longest.

A tall, good-looking surfer with long, bleached-blond hair stood next to Alissa. "Gnarly!" he jeered. "That was totally thrashin'!"

Blood trickled from Christy's elbow, stinging almost as much as her hurt pride. *This is the absolute worst moment of my entire life!* she wailed to herself.

Then one of the surfers, who had just ridden a wave into shore, came over to Christy. He planted his orange surfboard into the wet sand and reached out to help Christy untangle the seaweed from her ankle. "You okay?" It was more of a statement than a question.

"Yeah." Christy looked up into the face of the cutest guy she had ever seen. He matched exactly the description she had given to Paula months ago of "the perfect guy": sun-bleached blond hair falling across a broad forehead, a strong jaw, a straight nose, and screaming silver-blue eyes.

He took her by the elbow and helped her stand up.

"I feel so stupid," she confided softly.

He stood at least five inches taller, making her feel small.

"Yeah, I can see how you would." It didn't sound cruel the way he said it. He seemed to understand how she felt.

The others went back to their flirting with Alissa while Christy made her way through the hot sand to her towel. The cute guy tucked his orange surfboard under his arm and followed her. He just stood there while she dried herself off and tried to shake the sand from her ears.

Finally, Christy broke the silence. "Thanks for helping me."

"Sure," he said, carefully laying his board on Alissa's towel and sitting down next to it in the sand. "Will your friend mind if I borrow her towel?"

Christy glanced at her "friend," who was so involved in flirting with the surfers that she acted as if Christy didn't exist.

"I don't suppose so."

"I'm Todd." He smiled a fresh, clean smile.

"I'm Christy." She was surprised at how calm she acted around this unbelievably adorable guy. "Do you live here?"

"Yeah, during the summer—with my dad."

"Where's your mom?" Christy asked.

"Tallahassee."

"Where?"

"Florida. My parents are divorced, and my mom lives in Tallahassee. I live with her during the school year and spend the summers and some holidays with my dad."

Just then Alissa and one of the surfers sauntered over. They looked as though they were getting along very well. He had his arm around Alissa's waist, and they each held a beer bottle.

"You want some?" the guy offered Christy.

"No, that's okay," she answered, feeling caught off guard.

"Oh." He looked at Todd. "You must be one of his kind of friends."

"Well, actually, I brought some Cokes with me," she stammered, not sure what he meant by "one of Todd's friends."

"I've got two," she said, turning toward Todd. "Do you want one?"

"Sure."

Todd moved over next to Christy on her towel and then introduced the other surfer as Shawn. Christy introduced Alissa. Shawn moved Todd's board off the towel and sat down with Alissa beside him.

This is too wonderful to be true, Christy told herself. She knew her aunt would be thrilled.

For the next hour they sat and talked. Alissa pretty much carried the conversation. She had lots of stories about what life was like in Germany. Christy liked her accent, which must have been a combination of all the places Alissa had lived and all the languages she had been exposed to.

"And the cars go so slow on the autobahns here," Alissa said.

"But that's not the right word. What do you call them? Free-ways?"

"No," said Christy.

"Yeah," said Todd at the same time.

They looked at each other.

"In California we call them freeways," Todd explained.

"In Wisconsin we call them interstates," Christy said.

"You still drive very slowly here," Alissa said. "In Stuttgart, it was nothing to drive at 120 kilometers an hour."

Todd and Alissa talked about cars, and Christy listened. She barely knew the difference between a Jag and a Jetta and was afraid she might say something foolish. Shawn seemed quiet, too. He looked as though he wasn't all there, and his eyes were glazed. Whenever he did focus his gaze on Christy, she felt uncomfortable.

"Check it out," Shawn suddenly exclaimed, waving an arm toward the water. "That dude can shred!"

"What's that mean?" Christy asked Todd quietly.

"See that little kid out there on the white board? He's only about eight years old, and he's a really good surfer."

"How old are you?" Alissa asked Christy.

Thinking she was probably the youngest of the four of them, Christy started to lie. "Fifteen." But then she caught herself. "Well, actually, almost 15. My birthday is in a few weeks. How old are you?"

"Seventeen," Alissa answered.

Christy wasn't sure if she was lying or not. Alissa looked that old, but whenever she laughed, she seemed like a junior higher. Plus, why would she be hanging around someone as young as Christy if she really were 17?

"You guys haven't said how old you are," Alissa pointed out.

"Ah, I forget," Shawn said.

"We're both 16," Todd said.

"Thanks a lot," Shawn said. "Now she's going to leave because Alissa doesn't go out with guys who are younger than her, do you?"

"That all depends," Alissa said, giving Shawn a look that embarrassed Christy.

She wasn't sure why, but she felt as though she were intruding on a private game. Shawn must have known all the rules to this game, because he leaned over and whispered something to Alissa. Christy turned to look down toward the jetty.

"Waves are picking up," Todd said. "Let's go surfing, Shawn."

Shawn stood and offered Alissa his hand, pulling her up with him. "Naw. We're taking off," Shawn said.

Alissa grabbed her towel and slipped her hand into Shawn's. "See you guys later," she said. "Nice meeting you both." The couple moved quickly through the sand toward the row of beach houses.

"Are they going to get some lunch or something?" Christy asked, confused by their sudden exit.

Todd looked at her strangely. He didn't answer.

Christy wasn't sure what she had missed, but she knew Todd wasn't exactly thrilled about Shawn leaving. She didn't mind. She would love to spend the rest of the day sitting here, talking to Todd, looking into his gorgeous blue eyes. She had never liked a guy as much as she liked Todd, and she had only met him today! She wondered if he liked her. He seemed to, even though he hadn't tried to hold her hand or anything like Shawn had done with Alissa. Actually, the thought terrified her.

What if Todd tries to hold my hand? What if he tries to kiss me?

"Well, do you want to?" Todd interrupted her thoughts.

Christy's heart skipped a beat. "Want to what?" *Did he just read my thoughts?*

"Do you want to go surfing?"

"Oh!" Christy laughed. "I don't know. I'm not very coordinated in the water, as you may have noticed."

"I'll teach you."

"What I really want to learn is how to bodysurf. That's what Alissa was trying to teach me earlier."

"I'm not the best bodysurfer around, but I'll teach you what I know."

They dove into the water, and Christy was met again by that fresh exhilaration. Only this time it was magnified by the excitement of having Todd beside her. Like a pair of dolphins they faced the waves together, talking and laughing. Patiently Todd tried to teach her to bodysurf, but she couldn't get the timing right. Every wave rushed past her, taking Todd with it and leaving her behind, drenched.

After a while, another surfer paddled to where they were bobbing over the wave, and Todd introduced him as Doug. He was cute, and Christy thought he was much friendlier than Shawn and the other surfers she had encountered earlier.

"Try this," Doug said, offering Christy his body board.

"How do you use it?" Christy asked, unsure of what to do with the soft, short, blue and white board he held out to her. It was much shorter than a surfboard and looked less threatening.

"Well . . . you just hop on and ah, ah . . . I don't know! You hold on and ride it to shore," Doug said.

"Here," Todd offered. "I'll show her."

He strapped the Velcro end of a leash around his wrist. As the next wave swelled behind them, Todd lay across the body board on his stomach and began kicking furiously to get ahead of the wave. Christy and Doug floated over the wave and watched Todd as the wave broke right behind him, lifting him and the body board, pushing them to shore.

"Looks fun!" Christy exclaimed. "I think I can handle this."

"Sure you can!" Doug agreed. "Use it all you want."

"Thanks!"

Todd paddled back out and handed the body board to Christy. "Here you go. Remember to kick yourself ahead of the wave and hold on once it begins to carry you."

Christy self-consciously lay on the board. Todd and Doug's instructions and demonstrations suddenly eluded her. All she could think was, *I hope my rear end isn't sticking up!*

"Okay," Todd called out, "start kicking!"

Christy kicked and kicked and didn't look behind her. Suddenly, the force of the wave caught her, starting at her feet and then lifting her, pushing her upward, forward. Before she realized what was happening, the wave had enveloped her. As she hung on to the board for dear life, she felt the force of the ocean tide rushing toward the shore. For one triumphant moment, she felt as if she were flying. Then the belly of the body board slid onto the coarse sand at the shore, and immediately the wave receded.

Christy stood up, unscathed, and waved to Todd and Doug, who were waving their congratulations to her.

That was so fun! No wonder surfing is such a big deal. I can't imagine how it would feel to do that standing up on a board! Just lying on the body board was enough to take my breath away.

She fought the waves, getting back out to the calm swells where Todd and Doug were treading water.

"Awesome!" Doug said when she joined them.

"Awesome?" Todd echoed. "Nobody says 'awesome' anymore."

"I do!" Doug laughed. "And, Christy, that was an awesome ride! Took you all the way to shore." He had such a little boy look of joy on his tanned face that for a moment Doug reminded Christy of her little brother, David.

"Hey, what time do you think it is?" Todd asked.

"Probably close to 3:30," Doug said, squinting up at the angle of the sun.

"That's my guess, too. I gotta jam," Todd said. "I'm picking up Tracy from work."

Then he turned to Christy. "Will you be here tomorrow?"

Christy nodded her head, shivering a little from the cool water.

"Maybe you'll be ready to try surfing tomorrow," Todd said.

"Hey, this looks like a good one." Doug motioned toward the huge wave building behind them. "Let's all take it in."

While Christy lay on the body board, Doug and Todd held on to the sides, and they all kicked together. As soon as the wave caught up with them, the force tore the three of them apart, pushing Christy the fastest. She gave a tiny scream as the powerful surge thrust her forward, yanking the body board out from under her. She tumbled just once under the wave and came up behind it. The leash around her wrist allowed her to pull the board back. Todd and Doug, both now ahead of her, were rising out of the water at the shoreline.

Christy stretched back onto the board and let the wave behind her, a smaller and more tame one, gently nudge her to shore. She watched as Todd tilted his head back, shaking his sun-bleached hair so that all the salty droplets raced down his back.

"See you tomorrow," Doug called out as Todd headed up the beach toward where he left his surfboard in the sand.

"Yeah, later!" Todd called after them.

"You going back out in the water?" Doug asked Christy.

She was still watching Todd, hoping he would turn around and give one last wave meant only for her.

"No, I'm kind of cold," she said, unstrapping the Velcro leash around her wrist. "I think I'll lie out for a while. Thanks for letting me use your board. It was really fun!"

"Sure," Doug said, taking it from her. "Anytime."

Christy stretched out on her towel and let the warm sun bake her. The saltwater dried in little spots on her legs, and she felt scratchy and dry and terribly thirsty. She lasted on the towel only about half an hour before deciding she couldn't stand it any longer. Doug was still out in the water, riding his body board, and Todd wouldn't be back for the rest of the day. Alissa was long gone. There was no reason to wait around, so she gathered her belongings and hurried back to the house.

This whole day has been "awesome," to use Doug's word, she thought as she picked her way over the hot sand. *My aunt is going to be so proud of me! She was right. All I needed was the right kind of bathing suit and hairstyle. I love being part of Todd's group. Todd. Oh, man, Paula is never going to believe this!*

CHAPTER FIVE

The Invitation

Early the next morning, Christy marched out to the beach. Her hair washed and styled, her eye makeup in place, she anxiously looked for Todd. Except for a few surfers she didn't know, hardly anybody was on the beach. None of the group she had met the day before was there.

Slipping back into the silent house, she checked the clock: 8:27. No wonder nobody was on the beach yet. Christy dropped into a chair and snapped on the TV. A children's program was on. She sat there, numbly watching the brightly colored puppets as a green one with shifty eyes tried to talk a big, fuzzy yellow bird puppet into buying a pickle and sardine ice cream cone. The bird kept saying he didn't like it.

"How do you know you don't like it unless you try it?" The green puppet pressured his friend until he finally gave in, paid his quarter, and took a lick.

"Yeech!" The bird squawked. "I tried it, and I don't like it."

"Heh, heh, heh," laughed the green fellow. "I knew you wouldn't like it! But too bad for you because now I've got your quarter. Heh, heh, heh. You just made my day. Heh, heh, heh."

Oh, brother! thought Christy, clicking off the TV. *To think that that's supposed to be educational for little kids! Sheesh!*

"I tried it, and I don't like it," she mimicked in her puppet voice.

"Don't like what?" Uncle Bob's voice came from the doorway.

"Oh! A pickle and sardine ice cream cone."

"Then how about a pickle and sardine and cheese omelet?"

Christy laughed at her uncle's humor. "Okay—if you skip the pickles and the sardines!"

Over breakfast Christy talked with Uncle Bob about Todd. "He is the absolute cutest guy I've ever known, and I'm pretty sure he likes me."

"Any guy would be crazy not to like you, Christy."

Uncle Bob was so easy to talk to. Christy wished it could be the same way with her own dad, but he was a serious, hardworking farmer. Conversations with him consisted of him pondering a subject for hours, and then he'd tell Christy, "This is the way it is." Not much room for free thought or discussion. He was the dad, she was the daughter. He said, she did. That was that. She liked this feeling of being able to give her opinions, to talk things through, to feel capable of making wise decisions.

Her self-confidence lifted, she headed back out to the beach around 11:00, ready for anything. She was so exuberant that when she saw Todd, she ran to greet him, not realizing he was talking to another girl. A very cute girl.

"Hey, Christy," Todd called out. "How's it going? This is Tracy."

"Hi," Tracy said with a quick smile. Petite with shoulder-length light-brown hair, Tracy had a heart-shaped face that gave her a sweet, innocent look.

Christy's eyes darted from Todd to Tracy, then back to Todd. Had she intruded or what?

"Do you guys mind if I put my towel down here?"

"Of course not," Tracy answered. "Todd told me that two new

girls were out yesterday while I was at work. Is your friend coming?"

"I don't know. I just met her yesterday, and she took off with Shawn. I didn't see her the rest of the day."

"I saw them both this morning," Todd said in a low voice. "They'll probably be down later."

"I don't see how you can still be such tight friends with him," Tracy said to Todd.

"Shawn and I have been friends a long time."

"I know, but you guys don't have anything in common anymore."

"I can't just ignore him," Todd defended.

"Don't get mad," Tracy scolded. "I only wondered why you still do things with him, that's all."

"Where do you work?" Christy interjected, trying to clear the air. She couldn't quite tell if Todd and Tracy were talking to each other like brother and sister or like boyfriend and girlfriend.

"At Hanson's Parlor. It's an ice cream shop down by the Pavilion. Do you need a job? They're looking for someone else to work nights."

"No. But thanks anyway," Christy answered, still trying to discern Todd and Tracy's relationship. Todd and Tracy. Their names even went together! Did he like Tracy? She felt jittery, wanting to know where she stood with him.

"What time do you work today?" Todd asked Tracy.

"Noon to 6:00. Can you still give me a ride?"

"Sure. We probably should leave pretty soon. Hey, there's Shawn and Alissa."

Now Christy definitely felt like a fifth wheel. Shawn and Alissa came up with their arms around each other, clearly orbiting in their own private galaxy.

What am I doing here? Christy thought.

"Are you all coming to the party tomorrow night?" Alissa asked.

"What party?"

"Shawn's. His parents are going out of town for the weekend."

"Are you going, Tracy?" Christy asked.

"No. I'm not much of a party person. Besides, I've got to work."

"What about you, Todd?"

"I'll probably stop by."

Christy's interest rose. If Tracy wasn't there, maybe she would have a better chance with Todd.

"I guess I'll go," Christy said. "I'll have my aunt drop me off."

"Oh, you don't want to do that!" Alissa warned her with a light laugh. "Not for a party like this! It's only a few blocks. You can walk over with me, if you want."

"That would be great." Christy cast a glance at Todd to see if he would offer to pick her up instead.

"We have to go," was all Todd said. "I'm taking Tracy to work, and I told my dad I'd finish painting the front deck today."

"Bye!" Christy called out as Todd and Tracy left. "See you later!" She tried not to sound too disappointed that Todd wasn't going to spend the day with her.

Alissa and Shawn decided to leave, too, and walked off with their arms around each other. Alissa's bronzed body, like a magnet, drew glances from everyone she passed. Surely she knew everyone was watching, but she acted oblivious to the attention. Christy pulled out her paperback and tried not to get too depressed about being left alone so suddenly. As the afternoon sun slowly beat down on her back, she kept looking up every few minutes, hoping Todd would come back.

She couldn't figure him out. Yesterday he acted as if he really liked her, and then today he and Tracy acted like a married couple—arguing, him giving her a ride to work.

Where do I fit? she wondered. *At least he'll be at the party tomorrow night, and Tracy won't be there. I wish I could act the way Alissa does around guys. Then I would have a better chance at getting a guy like Todd to be interested in me.*

After several hours of making little progress in the book, she gathered up her belongings and hopped through the burning sand, wondering how Alissa could manage to walk so gracefully. Everything Alissa did was perfect. If only she could be like her.

The worst part about going back to her aunt and uncle's beach house was that she knew Aunt Marti would want a full report on the day, and there wasn't much to tell. Except the party invitation. At least she had that to look forward to.

Marti lay stretched out in a lounge chair on the patio, a tall iced-tea glass in her hand. She had on a black bathing suit with a purple sash around the waist and an oversized straw hat with matching purple sash. Only her legs were exposed to the sun. She was studying a tabloid magazine that had a picture of a movie star on the front and headlines that said something about "Genessa Seeks Revenge." For just a moment, Christy thought her aunt looked a little like the movie star on the front of the magazine.

"Oh, Christy!" Her aunt looked up, startled. "I didn't see you there! Tell me all about your day, darling. Was it as wonderful as yesterday?"

Christy skimmed over the details, leaving out the part about being left alone, and told her aunt about the party invitation.

Aunt Marti cooed proudly, "I knew you could get in with the popular crowd if you tried! What time should I drop you off at the young man's house?"

"Actually, Alissa is going to pick me up." Christy hoped her aunt wouldn't object and insist on driving her, since Alissa made it sound immature to have an adult drop you off.

"Well, we'll see." Then, with a look of terror, she added, "Oh dear! We'll have to go shopping to get you something nice to wear."

"But Aunt Marti, I got a whole new wardrobe just the other day, remember?"

"Yes, but we didn't get any real party dresses!" Aunt Marti seemed genuinely distressed.

"Party dresses? I don't think I should wear a dress, Aunt Marti. What if we play Twister, like we did at Paula's birthday party?"

"Twister?" Aunt Marti asked, appearing unfamiliar with the game. "And who is Paula?"

"My best friend back home. I'm just going to wear jeans."

To Christy's relief, her aunt backed off.

As Christy walked into the kitchen, Uncle Bob was taking a frozen package of hamburger out of the freezer.

"Holy mackerel!" he exclaimed when he saw Christy. "Are you ever sunburned!"

"Oh, really?" She seemed pleased. "I'm surprised I got any sun on my face. I think I was on my stomach almost all day."

"Here, little lobster," he said, handing her a tube of Aloe Vera gel. "Put this on after your shower, or you'll swell up like a tomato and scare all the guys away."

"I didn't scare them away at the beach today," Christy responded flippantly. "I even got invited to a party," she announced, opening the refrigerator and scanning the shelves for anything edible.

"My, my," Uncle Bob retorted, "aren't we the little social butterfly, all of a sudden! Will we have the honor of your presence at dinner tonight?"

"Yes, the party isn't until tomorrow night." Christy grabbed a spoon and started eating rocky road ice cream right from the nearly empty carton. Uncle Bob didn't seem to mind.

"Did Todd invite you to the party?"

"No, but he's going to be there," she told him as she finished off the ice cream. "The party is at Shawn's house, and I'm going with Alissa." Christy tossed the empty ice cream container into the trash and began going through the cupboards. "Is there anything to eat around here?"

"In a few hours, there'll be a Mexican fiesta served on the front patio," he said with a dramatic flair. "Shall I call you when it's ready?"

"*Si, si, señor!*" Christy called over her shoulder as headed for the guest room.

Not until she looked in the bathroom mirror did she see what Uncle Bob meant about her face being sunburned. Even the tops of her ears were burned! As she washed her hair, the water from the showerhead felt like a thousand piercing needles jamming into her back. It took a major effort to get dressed. Even the Aloe Vera gel hurt as she gently applied it to her shoulders.

Later, as the three of them sat down for dinner, Aunt Marti got a good look at Christy's red face. "Christy, darling! You're terribly sunburned! Didn't you take any sunscreen for your face today?"

"It's all right, Martha," Uncle Bob calmed her. "I gave her some Aloe Vera gel. She'll be fine."

"Now don't eat too much dinner, dear. You need to keep light on your feet for tomorrow night."

"Really, Martha!" Bob protested.

"Well, tomorrow night is going to be an important evening for Christy, and I only want to make sure she's at her best."

Christy didn't feel at her best when the important evening

arrived. She had gotten so sunburned the day before that she spent the entire day lying around the house, moaning, drinking ice water, and tolerating Aunt Marti as she smeared a variety of home-remedy concoctions on Christy's painful shoulders and back.

Christy wanted to go out on the beach to look for Todd, but her aunt wouldn't let her out of the house. So Christy spent the day thinking about him; imagining what it would be like the next time she saw him.

Around 4:00 she started going through her closet, trying to decide what to wear. Finally, she settled on a new pair of jeans and her new Winnie the Pooh T-shirt. It was the kind of outfit Paula would have worn, but Christy wished she had Alissa's phone number so she could call to see what she was going to wear. Alissa was so much more mature than Paula, and having lived all over the world, she knew more about life than any of Christy's friends at home.

Brushing her short hair, Christy thought of Alissa's long, beautiful hair and decided to let hers grow out again. By the time she turned 17, it might be as long as Alissa's. She tilted her head back in front of the mirror, imitating Alissa's laugh, trying to swish her invisible long mane.

"Whatever are you doing, dear?" Aunt Marti had been watching from the bedroom doorway.

"Oh!" Christy spun around, startled. "Just . . . nothing."

"Well, it's really about time for you to get ready for the party. Have you decided what to wear yet?"

Christy looked down at her outfit. "This. I'm going to wear this. I'm almost all ready."

Aunt Marti scrutinized the outfit. "I suppose it is your decision. I was just trying to help." She turned to go, switching her guilt tone to an overly cheery announcement, "Dinner's ready."

I can't stand this! Christy inwardly screamed. *First, all I hear from adults is how to grow up and be true to myself and make my own decisions. Then, every time I turn around, they remind me of how immature I am and how totally stupid my decisions are.*

Christy threw her hairbrush on the floor, swung the closet door open, grabbed her new sundress and yanked the T-shirt off. *Ouch!* Her sunburned skin tugged and throbbed from all the violent action. She burst into tears and threw herself on the bed until the raging in her head subsided.

"I don't care what she thinks," Christy said, gathering her composure. "I'm going to wear what I want to wear. And I am *not* going to cry like a baby anymore!"

Christy put the T-shirt back on, brushed her hair, and calmly walked down the stairs.

CHAPTER SIX

What's a Girl Like Me . . . ?

At the dinner table, Christy picked at her stir-fried vegetables quietly. Aunt Marti swung back into full control.

"I'm so anxious to meet your new friend Alissa. I'm really very proud of you, Christy darling, for making friends so quickly and receiving an invitation to a party. It's absolutely marvelous!"

Christy didn't even feel like going to the party now. But she started to perk up as Uncle Bob told the humorous story of how his golf cart broke down on the fifteenth hole that afternoon. By the time Alissa rang the doorbell, Christy felt happy again and ready for a fun time.

Aunt Marti instantly took to Alissa. "She's the epitome of perfection," Marti whispered to Christy after they'd invited Alissa to come inside. "And she's a marvelous model for you to pattern yourself after."

Christy had had other thoughts about Alissa and the party as soon as she had opened the door. Alissa wore a dress—a stunning white, very fashionable dress that showed off her tan. The living room filled with the fragrance of gardenias as she made polite conversation with Bob and Marti. Christy studied her inch by inch. Her makeup was perfect, and her gorgeous long blond hair was perfect—everything about Alissa was perfect! Christy hated her and, at the same time, would have given anything to be just like her.

As they walked the three blocks to Shawn's house, Alissa said, "I almost didn't come. Shawn! He's such a loser. So immature."

"I thought you guys were really starting to like each other."

"Is that what you thought?" Alissa seemed surprised. "He's a big baby. I've got better things to do than baby-sit little boys."

When they arrived, Alissa moved through the room with ballerina-like motions. First twirling to greet this person, then raising a slender arm to wave at that person.

Christy watched her in amazement as the throb of the blaring music made her heart pound. Neither Shawn nor Todd was around. Just a sea of unfamiliar spectators casually observing Alissa's performance. Alissa carried out her well-rehearsed play until she floated to the couch, where the most gorgeous guy in the room sat. Christy guessed he must be at least 20. With his bleached blond curls and scruffy goatee, he reminded Christy of a movie star Paula liked. She couldn't remember his name, but Paula had posters of him in her room.

Alissa obviously zeroed in on this guy as the one she wanted to spend her time with. Christy knew that was the last she'd see of Alissa all night. As Christy watched Alissa smile and flirt with the guy she felt intimidated, frightened, and painfully aware that she was the only one wearing jeans. All the other girls were dressed in stylish outfits. She felt like a three-year-old, quivering in the corner in her Winnie-the-Pooh T-shirt. How could she ever admit that Aunt Marti had been right about the clothes?

Sure enough, Alissa and her new boyfriend were rising from the couch and heading for the front door, laughing with their arms wrapped around each other.

Now Christy was mad—mad and frightened. Everything inside demanded she run out the door and keep running the three blocks back to Bob and Marti's house. But she couldn't make her feet move. She knew she wasn't ready to face her aunt and explain why she was home so early. And what about Todd? He was the real reason she had come to this party.

People stood around with their backs to her, talking and holding beer cans; a few people were smoking. No one gave her a second glance. Trying to calm herself, Christy decided that maybe she would fit in better if she had something to hold in her hand like everyone else. Then she could stand there, holding a can of Coke, and wait for Todd to show up. With all the courage she could muster, Christy left her corner and found her way into the kitchen.

"Excuse me," she said to one of the surfers standing by the refrigerator. "Is this where you get stuff to drink?"

He didn't answer, just pointed to the ice chests on the kitchen floor and took another sip from his beer can. Christy stuck her hand in the ice and started scrounging around for a can of Coke. All she could find was beer. She went to the second ice chest and found the same thing. She didn't think she wanted beer. She had tried some once at Paula's house when she was 10 and thought it tasted awful. How could anyone drink the stuff?

Another guy came into the kitchen and yelled toward Christy, "Hey, grab me two cold ones."

It startled her. He was the first person who had spoken to her since she had arrived.

"Do you know where Shawn is?" Christy asked.

He didn't seem to hear her over the music. She asked again, more loudly. "Do you know where Shawn is?"

The surfer helped himself to the drinks in the ice chest when Christy didn't respond to his request. He looked her over as if he were trying to remember where he had seen her before.

"Shawn's upstairs," he answered. Then he made the

connection. "Hey, did Alissa come?"

"Yes, but she already left." Christy had to shout the words as another song came on that was even louder. Then she asked, "Where upstairs?"

"Huh?"

"Where upstairs is Shawn?" She was yelling right into his ear.

"Huh?" He looked confused.

The music stopped suddenly, just as Christy was yelling, "I just want to ask Shawn if he has any Coke!"

The room fell completely silent. One of the guys said, "Whoa, baby. Party tonight!" The girl beside him laughed.

Why is everyone staring at me? Her heart pounded. *Do they think I'm a baby asking for Coke instead of beer?*

Hanging on to what little composure she had left, she headed up the stairs. She tapped on the first closed door, and a guy's voice hollered, "Go away!" A knock on the second door produced Shawn.

"Hi," she said, feeling totally stupid.

Shawn looked around behind her. "Where's Alissa?"

"She left with some guy." Christy's voice reflected her irritation at being left. Shawn, too, must have felt irritated with Alissa because he and let out a string of words that shocked Christy. How could they act so in love one day and despise each other the next?

"I really didn't mean to upset you, Shawn. I just wanted to find out if you had any Coke."

He gave her a startled look, just like the surfer downstairs had. Then without saying anything, he motioned for her to step into the room. Christy thought it was a funny place to keep soft drinks. Six other people were sitting around on the bed and floor of what she guessed to be his parents' bedroom. Todd wasn't one of the six people.

Nobody said anything to her, yet they weren't completely ignoring her, either. It was as if she had walked in on a private little clique, and for some reason she had been accepted without a word.

Shawn handed the guy by the nightstand a book of matches and then came over to Christy and in a rather low voice said, "The coke didn't come in. But this stuff is better than anything you usually get around here." Shawn held out a strange-smelling cigarette to Christy.

Everyone seemed to be looking at her. Beads of perspiration stung her sunburned forehead as the realization came over her, and she blurted out, "You mean, that's marijuana?"

"Yeah, I told you—the coke didn't come in."

"Oh!" Christy said, shocked. "I didn't mean . . . I was only . . . I was looking for something to drink!"

Shawn shook his head and turned away from her. The room suddenly felt very small, and the air was heavy with what smelled like thick incense. It made Christy feel light-headed, and she couldn't think of what to do next. She hated feeling so immature and inexperienced. Yet there was no way she wanted to stay with this group, no matter how welcomed they made her feel.

What would Alissa do? The room spun around her. The music from downstairs pounded through the soles of her feet, reaching all the way to her temples.

Shawn turned back around and eyed her through the tendrils of smoke that rose from the joint in his mouth. Then he nodded, taking the joint and offering it to her. Christy closed her eyes. The smoke filled her nostrils. All of a sudden she heard a voice from across the room say, "Hey, how's it going?"

It was Todd.

Christy was flooded with embarrassment! Why did Todd have to walk in at that very moment? Without a word, she rushed past

Todd, fled from the room, and dashed down the stairs. Desperately, she pushed her way through the crush of people who were drinking and laughing. The raging music taunted her all the way to the front door. Not until she'd run almost a block away did she let the tears fall.

I am just a big baby! she screamed to herself. Slowing to a walk, Christy tried to catch her breath.

Suddenly, someone from behind touched her sunburned shoulder. She turned with force, ready to swing at whoever it was.

"You going home now?" Todd asked gently.

She turned away and blinked back the tears. "I guess so."

"I'll walk with you." It was another one of his statements. Not a question or an invitation, just a fact. "Let's go this way," he added, heading toward the water.

Christy ran her finger under each eye, hoping to clear away any smudged mascara. Willingly she followed him, not sure of what might happen next and too unsure of herself to do anything else.

CHAPTER SEVEN

A Time to Cry

Christy and Todd walked through the soft, cool sand in silence. The sun had just set, smearing the sky with orange and pink swirls. Christy filled her lungs with the fresh sea air, anxious to cleanse the last hour from her mind. Todd kept his gaze fixed out at the ocean. Why had he come with her? She had been so naive about so many things at the party. Was being alone with Todd another unwise move? She didn't know whom she could trust anymore.

Todd interrupted her jumbled thoughts. "You want to sit over there on the jetty for a while?"

"I-I don't know. I guess so." She felt guilty for not trusting Todd. But it was too hard to try to make any decisions at the moment.

They sat in silence for a long time, the waves crashing just below their feet, spraying a fine mist on Christy's jeans. The air felt warm, but the dampness of the ocean spray made Christy shiver, so she pulled her legs up and wrapped her arms around them, as if giving herself a comforting hug. The tranquility of the ocean sounds at night and the fresh salt-laced air had a calming effect on Christy.

"So," Todd began. It was as if he had purposely allowed

Christy time to clear her head, and now he was ready to talk. "Not your usual kind of party, was it?"

"No," Christy admitted.

She turned to him and noticed for the first time what a gentle face Todd had. His personality was strong and direct. But when she looked at him in the twilight haze, she could see something tender in his eyes. What had started as a crush was becoming something deeper than she had ever felt for any guy before. She really, really liked him.

"Can I tell you something?" she ventured. It was important to her that Todd know what kind of girl she was. "I've never smoked any kind of cigarette before. I've never even seen or smelled marijuana! I thought the smell was nauseating."

"Is that why you turned it down?" asked Todd.

"No . . ." She hesitated a moment. "I mean, I thought about it for half a second because I thought that's what Alissa would do, and I felt so stupid just standing there. But then I guess I didn't because of my summer promise."

"Your summer promise?" Todd repeated.

"Before I came here this summer, my parents made me promise I wouldn't do anything I'd regret later."

"Sounds wise," Todd said. His voice deepened as he added, "Promises can change your life, you know. Most people don't realize it, but a promise can last forever."

It was silent again for a few minutes as Christy reviewed the evening's events in her thoughts before asking, "Do you like it?"

"Like what?"

"Marijuana. Do you smoke it a lot?" Christy's boldness surprised even her, but Todd wasn't the kind of guy who played flirty games.

"No. I used to. Sometimes. But I don't anymore."

"Why?"

Todd looked right at Christy. "Because I'm a Christian now."

Christy was completely startled. She never expected such a statement from a California surfer. "What does that have to do with it?"

"Everything."

"Well, I'm a Christian, too," Christy said, trying to recover from her surprise. "My whole family is. I was baptized when I was a baby."

"I was baptized right out there," Todd said, pointing to the ocean. "Last summer. July 27th."

"You're kidding!" Christy adjusted her position on the jagged rocks and sat up straight. "That's my birthday!"

Todd looked as though he was about to say something, but they were interrupted by a loud group of people coming toward them. It was the group from the party. Shawn was leading the way, whooping it up, making all kinds of loud noises with an echo of support from the others. The traveling party stopped on the beach a short distance from Todd and Christy. Shawn yelled something about surfing the jetty with his eyes closed.

"What's he doing?" Christy asked.

"He's stoned. I've seen him like this before. He totally goes into the ozone. Looks like he's going bodysurfing, which is really stupid. Wait here. I'll be right back."

Christy couldn't hear Todd as he confronted Shawn, but she saw him pulling on Shawn's arm. Then she saw Shawn jerk away from Todd, and heard him bellow out a series of cuss words, ending with, "I don't need this from you! Get outta my face."

Shawn plunged into the water while a few of the guys in the crowd started pushing Todd around. He turned away from them and stalked through the sand back to Christy.

With his voice filled with tension, Todd shouted at Christy, "Hanson's is still open. You want to go?"

"Sure. Where?" Christy couldn't remember where she had heard that name before.

"Get some ice cream."

"Okay," Christy said, hopping down and falling into step with his brisk march. "What about Shawn?"

"Hey, I tried, okay? He's responsible for his own actions."

His words brimmed with anger and frustration, which made Christy pull back. With all her heart she wanted to slip her hand into his and give it a comforting squeeze. But she was too shy. Instead she chattered away, trying to use her words to cheer him up as they walked the nine blocks to the ice cream parlor.

"My uncle played golf today, and the funniest thing happened! His golf cart broke down, and he walked all the way back to the clubhouse before he realized he had left his clubs back in the cart at the 15th hole."

Todd's response was minimal. Obviously, it was much funnier when Uncle Bob told it. Todd remained solemn until they entered Hanson's Parlor. Suddenly he perked up, and Christy's heart sank when she realized why. Tracy worked here. And there she was, balancing a banana split in one hand and a malt in the other.

"Tracy! How's it going?" Todd ambled over to a table with Christy close behind.

"Hi, you guys! I'll be with you in just a second." Her hair, pulled up in a ponytail, was tied with a bright pink ribbon that matched the ruffled apron of her uniform. She looked too cute.

Christy sank into the chair and watched Tracy gingerly deliver two huge hot-fudge sundaes to the table next to theirs. Then, wiping her hands on her apron, Tracy stepped over and said, "It's been so busy tonight! If you had come an hour earlier, there wouldn't have been a place to sit."

"What do you want, Christy?" Todd asked, his steady manner returning.

Christy decided to play it coy in front of Tracy. "I don't know, Todd. I didn't bring any money with me."

"Don't worry, I've got enough. As long as you don't order the 'Hanson's Extravaganza.' "

"Oh, please!" Tracy moaned. "Making two of those in one night is more than I can handle, and I've already reached my quota!"

"Then I'll have a hot-fudge sundae with chocolate chip ice cream and no nuts," Christy ordered.

"And I'll have my usual," Todd said, smiling at Tracy.

Christy tried to subdue her feeling of jealousy over Todd and Tracy's closeness because at this very moment, she realized she was on what could actually be considered her first real date. She and Paula had a contest, now into its fourth month, to see who would be the first to go out on a real date. The rules were that the guy had to ask, he had to pay, and he had to be the one to take you home. Christy had two out of three so far. It looked as though Paula would have to be the one to cough up the $10.

Todd's "usual" turned out to be a mango shake with a pineapple wedge. Tracy placed the ice cream on the table with much more grace than Christy knew she could have managed and asked, "Weren't you going to Shawn's party, Christy?"

"I went, but there wasn't much going on, so, ah, I left." *Why did I make it sound like that? What if Todd tells her the real story of how I ran out of the house, crying?*

"That's not exactly the whole story," Todd told Tracy.

Christy felt so foolish.

"It really ticks me off, Tracy. When we left, Shawn was totally stoned. I tried to stop him from going into the water, but he just blew me off like I was nothing to him." Todd took a chomp out of his pineapple wedge. "I almost slugged him, Trace. I almost bashed him right in the face. But I know it wouldn't have stopped him."

Christy felt excluded from the conversation as Tracy gave her advice to Todd. "I know it's hard, Todd, but you can't spend the rest of your life feeling responsible for Shawn. He's the one in the wrong. It's not your problem. Just turn it over to the Lord."

Todd's response held the same brother-sister argumentative spirit Christy had seen between the couple on the beach. "But he's my best friend! I can't just let it go like I don't care! You've never understood that about me, Tracy. I stick up for my friends, even when they're being jerks."

Tracy excused herself. "I have to go take some more orders."

"So . . ." Christy tried to break into the conversation. "You and Shawn are really close friends?"

"Yeah. We've known each other a long time and we used to do everything together, and I mean everything. But last summer when I became a Christian, we kind of went our separate ways. I wasn't into all the stuff he was into anymore. Except surfing."

Christy didn't understand why "becoming a Christian," as Todd said, would change anything between friends.

Todd remained withdrawn when he walked Christy home. She fought the sinking feeling inside that maybe he didn't like her the same way she liked him. But at the front door her spirits rose.

"I want to get your phone number," Todd said in his matter-of-fact way.

"7–9–4—" She stopped, realizing that was her home phone. She didn't know her aunt and uncle's number.

"Just a minute," she said, leaving Todd by the front door while she ran in to copy the number off the kitchen phone.

When she returned, an ambulance siren blared a few blocks away. It was so loud that Christy could barely hear what Todd said as he waved good-bye. Did he say, "I'll see you tomorrow" or "I'll call you tomorrow"? Either way, Christy's excitement soared as she met Aunt Marti in the living room.

"Well, Christy my dear! I'm dying to hear all about your party. Did you and Alissa have a good time? What did you have to eat? Did you play Twister like you thought you would?"

Christy laughed and laughed.

"I don't understand," her aunt said. "Why are you laughing, dear?"

Christy stretched out on the plush carpet and shook her head. "Let me just say that it wasn't the kind of evening I thought it would be. But I ended up having a good time anyway, and Todd brought me home. He might call me tomorrow, so I better tell Uncle Bob not to give him a hard time."

"Whatever do you mean, Christy?" Aunt Marti asked, blinking her eyes. "Your uncle would never do anything to embarrass you!"

"Oh, right!" Christy laughed all the way up to her room. What a night! What a week! She felt as if she had grown up and changed more in the last few days than she had in the last three years.

When she woke up the next morning, Christy still felt exuberant. Cleansing her face and putting on her makeup, she thought about Todd. Should she go down to the beach or wait around for him to call? With special care, she curled her hair and was nearly finished when Uncle Bob knocked on her door.

"Christy—telephone! Somebody named Rod or Claude or Schmod or something."

"Eeeeeeee!" Christy squealed. "I'll be right there!"

With one last look in the mirror, she took the stairs two at a time and picked up the phone in the den.

"I've got it, Uncle Bob," she hollered and then heard a considerate click.

"Hello?" She tried to sound aloof yet interested and at the same time charming. Even though Todd didn't seem the type to play these kinds of games, why couldn't she?

"Christy. It's Todd. I'm at the hospital. Do you think your aunt or uncle could bring you over? It's Hoag Memorial."

Christy was so shocked she nearly dropped the receiver. "Todd! What—how—what happened? Are you all right?"

"It's not me," he assured her. "It's Shawn. He crashed into the jetty last night. Broke a lot of bones. Lost a lot of blood. He's still unconscious."

"When did you find out?"

"Last night when I left your house. There was an ambulance out on the beach. I had a feeling it must be Shawn, so I followed them to the hospital. I've been here all night. His parents are out of town. I thought I'd go back to his house and try to find some phone numbers of relatives or somebody who might know where they are." The weariness showed in his voice.

"Well, what can I do?" Christy felt shocked and helpless, but willing to do anything for Todd.

"I wondered if you could be with him in case he comes to. He might be able to tell you where his parents are. I wouldn't have called you except I couldn't get ahold of anybody else."

"Sure, Todd," Christy responded numbly. "I'll come right over."

Uncle Bob drove as Aunt Marti chattered nervously. Todd met them in the lobby and told them what room to go to and the phone number to Shawn's house. He looked pale and distraught. The expression looked out of place on his strong, gentle face. Christy wished she could throw her arms around him, hug him, and cry on his shoulder.

Todd left, and the three of them rode the elevator to Shawn's floor. Then so many things happened at once that it was hard to figure out what was going on. Shawn had stopped breathing and was taken immediately to the operating room. There was some kind of problem over Shawn's being under 18 and his parents not being there to sign release papers for the surgery. Uncle Bob spoke in hushed tones with the doctor while Aunt Marti and Christy stood in the hallway. From out of nowhere a police officer appeared, and a nurse directed him to Christy.

"Excuse me, miss," he said, peering intently at her. He was a large man and his mere presence startled Christy. "I'm Officer Martin. May I ask you a few questions?"

"Yes, sir."

"Were you with Shawn Russell last night at the time of the accident?"

"Yes. I mean no. I mean sort of," Christy floundered.

"I see," said Officer Martin, raising an eyebrow. "Perhaps we should sit down, and you should tell me what you know."

Aunt Marti was the first to sit down, nervously clicking her nails. "Now tell him everything, Christy darling." Her voice was higher and squeakier than usual.

"Well, there was a party at Shawn's house last night, and I got there about 8:00," Christy began.

"Were there drugs at this party?"

Aunt Marti gasped. "Heavens, no!"

The officer looked irritated. "Perhaps you can let the young lady answer for herself."

Aunt Marti recoiled in her seat.

Christy's heart pounded. "Yes, sir."

"There were drugs?" he repeated.

"Yes, sir." Out of the corner of her eye, she could see Aunt Marti turning pale. "I went upstairs," Christy told him, her voice shaking, "because one of the guys told me to go upstairs. See, I was trying to find something to drink besides beer, and I asked if they had any Coke, and they told me to go upstairs and ask Shawn. Shawn Russell. It was at his house. The party, I mean.'' She was shaking so badly she could hardly think straight.

"Go on," the officer instructed.

"Well, I went upstairs to the bedroom, and when I went in, there were some people and they were, well, I didn't know what they were doing at first. But then I figured out it was drugs. They were smoking marijuana."

"Oh!" Aunt Marti looked as if she might faint.

"Miss Miller," the officer bent down and looked forcefully at Christy, "did you participate in the use of any illegal drugs last night?"

"No!" The word jumped out of her throat like a scared cat. Then pulling back she said, "No, sir, I did not."

Never before in her life had she felt so good. So glad she had made the right decision.

Aunt Marti heaved a huge sigh of relief.

"Do you know the names of any of the other people at the party?" the officer asked.

"Just Todd. I think his last name is Spencer, but I'm not sure. He's the guy who is at Shawn's house trying to locate his parents."

"And you honestly did not know any of the other people in the bedroom last night?" He didn't seem convinced.

"No, sir."

"Okay, go on."

Christy gave him a few more details. Then he stopped her and questioned, "Now Todd was the one with you when you left the beach after Shawn headed for the water."

Christy nodded.

"Did Todd try to stop Shawn from going into the water?"

"Yes, sir. But it was no use. He said Shawn was too stoned to know what was going on. Some of the other guys started pushing Todd around. I was afraid there might be a fight."

Christy noticed Uncle Bob walking back down the hall toward them, his face stone-gray. He walked over to Christy and cupped her chin in his hand.

"I'm sorry, honey." Tears filled his eyes. "There was nothing the doctors could do."

"Oh, dear me!" gasped Aunt Marti.

"The patient expired?" asked the officer with no emotion in his voice.

Uncle Bob nodded.

"Well, thank you for your time, Miss Miller," the policeman said, briskly excusing himself.

Uncle Bob sat down and slipped his arm around Christy. She began to shake uncontrollably and cried into his light-blue golf shirt, leaving streaks of mascara on the shoulder.

"Todd doesn't know!" she cried. "We've got to call him. Where's the number?"

Aunt Marti had regained her composure and was back in control of things. "Now, Christy, let your uncle call him. You stay here and calm yourself."

Christy's mind raced through its crazy maze while Uncle Bob stood at the phone booth a few yards away. How could Shawn be dead? She just met him a few days ago, and now he was gone. It couldn't be true. The tears flowed down her cheeks.

Uncle Bob returned and said softly, "I think we'd better go now."

"What about Todd?" Christy sobbed.

"I got ahold of him. He had tracked down Shawn's parents. They were staying with friends in Carmel but are taking the next flight back. Todd will pick them up at the airport." Then he added gently, "They don't know yet."

The drive home was uncomfortable. Except for Christy's sniffling and Aunt Marti's occasional deep sighs, all was quiet. Just as they pulled into the driveway, Aunt Marti broke the silence.

"Actually, Christina, I had no idea these were the kinds of friends you had been keeping company with! Why, if I thought for one minute that you were going to a drug party last night, I—"

Uncle Bob cut her off with a force Christy had never seen from him. "Martha, let it go! I mean it! Don't you dare say another word to her. Can't you see you're the one who pushed her into all this?"

"Me? How did I push her?"

"Yes, you! And you're too stubborn to admit it! You wouldn't let Christy stay innocent. You had to try to give her whole life a makeover and the truth is, she didn't need it!" With that he slammed the car door and stormed into the house.

"Well!" Aunt Marti was indignant. "I don't know where that came from!"

Christy wasn't sure what she should do. She had never seen them fight like this before.

In the same way that a foaming wave recedes, Aunt Marti's anger disappeared, and her cool composure returned. "Christy dear, don't mind your uncle. I'm sure he didn't mean to hurt you. Why don't you and I go out for a salad over on Balboa Island? There's a marvelous little place I've been wanting to take you."

It seemed to Christy that the whole world was spinning around her. How could Aunt Marti talk about eating? She stared at her aunt. What a cold, insensitive woman! Did she think that ignoring reality would make it go away?

"Shall we go?" Aunt Marti prodded, fumbling for her keys.

Christy responded with all the graciousness she could find in her troubled spirit. "To be honest, Aunt Martha, I don't feel much like eating. I'd rather go lie down for a while—if that's okay with you." The ending came out as sarcastic as it was meant to.

Aunt Marti stiffened. "Fine. I'll just go by myself, then."

Christy pulled herself out of the car and somberly opened the front door as the silver Mercedes lurched from the driveway and sped down the street. A pounding ache crashed against the insides of Christy's head. She retreated to her room, where she spent the rest of the day with the door closed. For a long while she lay on her bed, staring at nothing. Like a scratched CD that skipped back to the same place over and over again, Shawn's death would not stop playing itself over in her head.

So many thoughts pierced her. Why Shawn? He was only 16. Sure, he had been smoking dope, but it was still an accident. Couldn't God have kept it from happening? We all make mistakes. And where was Shawn now? Was he in heaven or . . . Was hell a real place? Do people really go there when they die? How could he have died, just like that? It didn't seem real. Nothing seemed real. Maybe if she could write everything out, take a look at all the events of the past few days on paper, they might make sense—or at least stop spinning around in her head.

She wrote everything out in a letter to Paula. It took hours, and her hand cramped from holding the pen so tightly.

"Christy?" her uncle called softly from the other side of her closed door.

She glanced up from her stationery pad.

"You want me to get you anything?" he asked.

"No, thanks."

"Anything to drink? Are you hungry at all?"

"No. I'd like to be alone, if that's okay."

"Sure," he said. "I won't bother you again. But be sure to holler if you want anything. Anything at all. Okay?"

"Okay. I will. Thanks."

She continued writing. It was the longest letter she had ever written. Twelve pages on both sides. Yet, as she reread it, the answers she was looking for weren't there.

The sun was starting to set when she looked out her window. Everything in the outside world went on. The waves kept coming in and rolling out. The seagulls kept circling the trash cans. The joggers arrived for their evening jog, right on schedule. Nothing stopped. Life kept going for everyone else. It didn't seem right.

Finally, the fatigue of the day overtook her. She went into the bathroom, soaked a washcloth with warm water, and held it against her face, breathing in the steam. Everything seemed harsh and severe. Even the washcloth felt coarse and prickly.

She barely knew Shawn, and yet she was overwhelmed with emotion. *What would it be like*, she thought, *if the death had happened to someone I was really close to?*

She stumbled into bed, pulled the comforter tightly around her shoulders, and fell into a deep, deep sleep.

CHAPTER EIGHT

Questions and Answers

The next few days passed like a mist over the ocean. It was as if Christy knew things were happening, but all she could see were faint outlines, distorting the true forms of things. Nothing was clear or in focus.

Uncle Bob and Aunt Marti had reconciled after their tiff and had both come to Christy with their apologies. Aunt Marti laughed it off, while Uncle Bob's words flowed with genuine concern for Christy's feelings.

Aunt Marti suggested they fly to San Francisco for a few days. She wanted to leave the next day and had already made airline arrangements. But with Uncle Bob's help, Christy persuaded her to take a later flight so Christy could go to Shawn's funeral.

The day of the funeral she stood in front of her closet for the longest time, trying to decide what to wear. She had only been to two funerals before, but they were for old people and were too long ago for her to remember what she wore. She didn't have any idea what would be appropriate. She finally decided on the old skirt and long top she wore the day she and Aunt Marti had gone shopping. Maybe it wasn't stylish, but it was familiar and felt more secure than her new clothes.

Meeting Uncle Bob in the kitchen, Christy discovered that

Aunt Marti had prepared her a protein drink for breakfast and was busy packing for their trip. Only Uncle Bob accompanied her to the funeral. Neither of them said much in the car. When Bob parked in front of the stark white colonial-style mortuary, Christy had a strong desire to ask her uncle to turn the car around and go home. But there on the front steps stood Todd and Tracy. Christy hadn't seen Todd since that morning in the hospital, and he had called only once to tell her the time and place of the funeral. She sucked in a deep breath and headed for the steps.

Todd smiled when he saw her. "I'm really glad you came, Christy."

He looked exhausted. Christy wanted to cry, but instead she boldly held out her arms and let Todd fall into her embrace. They held each other for a long time. Then, without words, they pulled apart, and Tracy gave her a strong hug while Bob and Todd shook hands.

They shuffled into a small room, glutted with monstrous flower arrangements. The air seemed to push against Christy's chest, choking her with its pungent sweetness. Organ music, slow and monotonous, pounded the insides of her head. She wanted to throw up.

A bald clergyman, wearing a black robe, delivered a short message. Shawn's mother sat in the front row, sobbing all the way through. Then a large, red-haired lady in a dark gray dress sang a morose song, clasping her hands together as if this were an opera rather than a funeral.

The clergyman stepped back onto the podium, announcing that one of Shawn's closest friends had asked to say a few words. With his firm, sure manner, Todd walked to the front. He looked confident, but Christy noticed his hands were shaking.

"I've been friends with Shawn for a long time," he began and then paused to clear his throat. "I was there the night he died, and I'll probably never forgive myself for not doing more to stop him." His voice cracked. "We were really tight. We did everything together until last summer, when I became a Christian. I really wanted Shawn to become a Christian, too. I don't know if he ever did."

That's when Todd broke. He let out a deep, choking sob and quickly wiped his eyes with the palms of his hands. Christy blinked away her own tears and looked over at Tracy. Tears streamed down Tracy's face. She didn't even try to stop them.

Uncle Bob touched Christy's arm gently, offering her his handkerchief. She looked up at his face to signal her thanks and was startled to see how controlled he seemed. None of the emotion Bob had expressed at the hospital now showed on his face.

Todd was standing still, his head down, his jaw clenched, trying hard to get back in control. The clergyman had stepped back onto the podium and was motioning for Todd to sit down. Todd wiped his tears away and held up a moist palm as if to say, "Just a minute." He drew in a deep breath and said, "I want to read something. I . . ." He cleared his throat. "I found a verse in the Gospel of John that has helped me."

With trembling hands, Todd leafed through his Bible. When he found the verse, he placed his Bible on the podium and looked up. His eyes misted with tears all over again.

"It's in chapter 11. One of Jesus' closest friends died, and what blows me away is that Jesus cried. It says here that Jesus wept. It's okay for us to be upset when someone we love dies." Todd brushed away his trickling tears and kept going. "But the part I want to read is what Jesus said to His friend's family. He said, 'I am the resurrection and the life; he who believes in Me shall live even if he dies.' "

Closing his Bible, Todd looked over at Shawn's parents. His

eyes were clearer, but Christy couldn't believe how pale he looked.

"What I want to say is that I wish I had this whole last week to live over again. I wish Shawn were still alive. I wish he'd believed in Jesus and turned his life over to Him."

Todd squeezed his eyes closed, as if trying hard to find the right words. "I'm not making this very clear, but I know that Jesus radically changed me. All I did was pray and ask Him to forgive my sins and take over my life. I just totally believed. And now I know I'm going to spend eternity with Him in heaven. I just wish . . ." He choked up again. "I wish Shawn . . . I wish all of you . . ."

Todd couldn't finish. He grabbed his Bible, stepped down from the podium, and shakily made his way back to the pew. Covering his eyes with his hands, Todd wept.

Christy thought she couldn't stand it another second. The clergyman stepped forward and, in a deep, controlled voice, offered a lofty-sounding benediction. The group dispersed. Many were sniffling and most looked down rather than at the people around them.

Christy walked briskly to the car, swallowing back the tears. She wanted to leave—now. No way could she go to the gravesite. Bob didn't even ask. He drove home in silence.

Not until Christy was on the plane to San Francisco, looking out the window at the Pacific Ocean below, did she release the emotion she had choked down at the funeral. Turning her face to the window, she let the tears flow. Through bleary eyes, she tried to focus on the miniaturized California coastline below. From up here, the waves looked like a thin line of soap suds. Harmless. Soft and foamy. How could those same waves have taken Shawn's life? Is this how God sees everything? From such an exalted distance that it all looks insignificant? Unimportant? Did He really care about how people felt? Then she remembered what Todd had said, "Jesus wept." God must care.

"Christy—" Aunt Marti interrupted her thoughts as she tapped Christy on the shoulder. "I have something to say to you, dear. You mustn't get all worked up about this funeral. Your parents raised you to be a nice Christian girl, and you don't need to dwell on ugly things like death."

Christy glared at her aunt. *How can you simplify all of life like that to make it fit in your compact Gucci bag? There has to be more to life than money and clothes and being popular and all the other things you've drilled me on.* She reclined her seat with a jerk and put the headphones on, letting the beat of the music pound away her heavy thoughts.

Christy felt like a robot, moving through the San Francisco airport and into the taxi that took them to the St. Francis Hotel. Her head ached, and her jaw hurt from clenching her teeth. She should have been awed and impressed with the plush carpet, high ornate ceiling, and tinkling chandeliers of the hotel lobby. She should have been taking mental notes so she could tell Paula all about it. But she didn't care. She dejectedly stood to the side, waiting for Aunt Marti to check them in. Christy fingered her purse strap and tried to close her ears to all the commotion around her. People spoke in foreign languages, bellhops bumped luggage onto wheeled carts, and from the other end of the lobby, someone played a piano in one of the hotel restaurants.

As soon as they got to their suites, 1133 and 1134, Uncle Bob opened his bag and pulled out aspirin for Christy.

"These should help," he offered and then retreated to his and Marti's adjoining suite.

Christy unwrapped the glass in her bathroom and filled it with water. She swallowed the aspirin and looked herself over in the mirror. She didn't look too great. Swollen, red eyes. Downturned mouth. Even her hair looked droopy. She didn't feel too great, either.

Walking around her big room, Christy touched the glass door-knobs and smoothed her hand over the velvety, salmon-colored love seat. Then, pulling back the heavy drapes, she looked down on Union Square just as Bob knocked on the door.

"Ready to see the sights?" he asked, walking in with Marti right behind him. Marti had changed clothes, and the room filled with the fragrance of her perfume.

"Are those all department stores out there?" Christy asked, pointing out the window at the tall buildings that framed the park in the middle of Union Square.

"Yup," Bob said. "Why do you think we always stay at the St. Francis?"

"The Macy's over there is wonderful," Marti added, pointing to the right. "But we'll have to shop at I. Magnin, Nordstrom, and Saks as well."

"Wow!" Christy exclaimed, "I've never seen so many big stores—and all in one spot."

"Come on," Uncle Bob suggested. "Let's go for a cable-car ride."

Even though it was mid-July and only 4:00 in the afternoon, they all took jackets. After a 40-minute wait, they pushed their way through the crowd onto the cable car and headed for Fisherman's Wharf. Christy stood on the outside, her arm looped around the pole. The cable car jerked and swayed as the underground cables pulled it up the steep hill and pointed it toward the bright blue bay ahead. Breathless, Christy held on to the pole for dear life. What a ride! And what a festive feeling in the air! Did it come from all the tourists chatting with each other on the cable car? Or from the brisk wind chasing them down the hill? Perhaps it was the way all the houses they passed looked like something from a Victorian storybook, making the cable-car ride seem even more enchanting and fanciful, as though it was taking them into a fairy tale. Whatever it was, Christy's exhilaration was quite evident to Aunt Marti.

"Didn't I tell you, Bob?" she whispered to Bob. They were seated on the wooden bench seat of the cable car, directly behind Christy. "Poor thing merely needed to get away from all that stress. It's not good for a girl her age. Might cause premature wrinkles, you know!"

Uncle Bob smiled his agreement and then turned to the cable-car driver, who was standing directly behind him, working the levers with his strong, gloved hands.

"You took that corner quite well," Bob noted. "You been doing this long?"

"Yes, sir," replied the large African-American man, who wore a jaunty beret and snappy brown uniform, "ever since 1985 when they opened the lines back up. They were closed down for refurbishing for two years, you know."

"Yeah, I remember hearing that." Bob seemed genuinely interested.

"We're pretty proud of our system. It's the only working cable-car line in the world," the driver said.

"It sure is fun!" Christy yelled as the driver rang the brass bell. Ding-ding-ding-ding. Christy laughed aloud.

"Hold yourself in there, young lady!" the driver warned. "We're passing another cable car."

Christy pulled her torso in until her stomach pressed hard against Aunt Marti's knees. The other car brushed past them, and Christy could feel the bump of a shoulder bag from someone hanging on to the passing car.

"That was close!" Christy exclaimed.

Uncle Bob squeezed her arm. "Glad to see the smile back on

your face. What do you want to do? Eat first or browse through all the tourist traps?"

"Let's browse a bit first, don't you think, dear?" It was evident that Aunt Marti had already set an itinerary in her mind. "Bob, you can go check on your fishing boat, and then at say 6:30, we'll meet you at Alioto's for dinner."

"Sounds good," Uncle Bob obliged, and as the cable car came to a stop, they stepped off and went their separate ways.

"These little places are rather junky," Aunt Marti whispered to Christy as they entered a small souvenir shop. "But I thought you might find a trinket to take home. Tomorrow we'll do some real shopping in the heart of the city. Now, when you see something you like, you let me know."

Christy picked up a small, brightly colored music box with a cable car that moved up and down a ceramic hill as it played "I Left My Heart in San Francisco."

"Look, how cute!" Christy exclaimed.

Aunt Marti caught the cashier's attention. "Do you have a box for this, and could you pad it well for us?"

The cashier carefully wrapped the music box as Christy softly hummed the familiar tune. *Actually*, she thought, *I left my heart in Newport Beach*. She dreamt of how wonderful it would have been to stand next to Todd on the cable car and to feel his arm around her as they rolled down the hills.

Aunt Marti brought her back to reality as they hailed a bicycle cab and rode in the rickshaw-type seat down to Pier 39. Bright, fluttering kites flew high in the summer evening sky while a variety of street performers gathered crowds. Christy found herself fascinated with a juggler who tossed meat cleavers into the air, but Aunt Marti was quite insistent about moving along.

They entered a shop specializing in every kind of Christmas ornament imaginable. Aunt Marti had had a sudden inspiration to pick a theme for her Christmas tree and buy all the ornaments now. After much deliberation, she chose lambs rather than angels and selected enough to fill an entire tree.

"I'll be at the register, Christy." She seemed quite pleased with herself. "Find anything you would like?"

"I'm not sure yet." Christy toyed with the ornament in her hand—a wooden teddy bear with the name "Todd" painted in fancy black letters. Except for her dad and brother, Christy had never bought anything for a guy before. She really wanted to get something for Todd. But a teddy bear ornament? What would Todd think of such a gift?

"Well, dear?" Aunt Marti called from the register, where she filed through her credit cards.

"No," Christy replied, putting the ornament back. "I didn't find anything here. Maybe at the next store."

The next store turned out to be a sweatshirt shop. Hanging from long wooden pegs on the walls was an incredible display of every color and size imaginable.

"This one's great!" Christy said, holding up a black and white sweatshirt with bold letters across the front saying, "ESCAPED FROM ALCATRAZ."

"Well . . . " Aunt Marti wasn't convinced. "It's not very feminine, dear, but if that's what you want, I guess—"

"No," Christy said and laughed, "it's not for me! For Todd. Can I get it for him? Please?"

"I see." Aunt Marti surveyed the sweatshirt. "Yes, I suppose that would be all right. Why don't you pick one out for yourself, too, dear. That blue one with the white sailboat is darling, don't you think?"

No, Christy didn't think the blue one was darling. She considered getting an "Alcatraz" sweatshirt for herself as well, so she and Todd could show up at the beach in matching shirts. But that seemed like something Paula would do, and not what Christy could see herself doing.

Twenty minutes later, they were sitting at a window booth in Alioto's, buttering warm sourdough bread and watching the misty fog creep in on the bay. Christy ordered crab legs, something she had never eaten before. Carefully, she cracked them and pulled the steaming, tender white meat from each leg, dipping it in the drawn butter. What a feast!

She was wiping her hands with the white cloth napkin when Uncle Bob interrupted Marti's chitchat to become philosophical with Christy.

"There are many things in this life to experience, Christy. It's okay to experience anything you want as long as you know when to pull back. Do you know what I'm saying?"

"I'm not sure." Actually, she was completely lost.

"It's like the cable-car ride," Uncle Bob explained. "You were having a great time riding on the outside, hanging on and feeling the full force of the wind and the momentum of the cable car. But then you pulled yourself in, just in time, when we slid past the other car. And you were safe."

"What are you trying to tell me?" Christy asked, popping the last bit of crab into her mouth.

"Just what I've told you before. Be true to yourself. Do what you want to do. Be your own person. Make the most of your life because it's your life. That's what I'm trying to say."

For once Aunt Marti remained silent as Christy bluntly replied, "But Uncle Bob, Shawn did what he wanted to do. He was his own person. And now he's dead."

It was silent for a moment, and then Bob answered. "That's exactly what I meant about the cable car." He leaned across the table to make his point. "You just have to pull yourself in at the right time, and you won't get hurt."

"I don't know," Christy countered. "I'm not sure I want to live on the edge like that. I mean, what about God? Where does He fit in? Does He just let me go my own merry way, and if I don't happen to 'pull myself in' in time, then splat-splat, that's that, too bad, Christy?" She sat back in her seat.

Aunt Marti seemed embarrassed that they were discussing these things in a restaurant and tried to wrap up the conversation in her own compact way. "Of course not, dear. God is love. Everybody knows that. God helps those who help themselves. All you need to do is try to be a good person, just like Bob and I have always done."

"Yes, but Aunt Marti," Christy said, "are you sure that's all there is to it? For instance, how do you know for sure that you're going to heaven when you die?"

Aunt Marti bristled. "I don't think this is either the time or the place to get into a theological discussion, Christina." Then turning to Bob, she added, "Pay the bill, will you, darling? I'm going to the ladies' room."

It felt as if an icy wind had blown across the room as Marti left the table. Christy sensed the haze of the previous days closing in around her. She might be young, naive, and inexperienced, but she knew she wasn't stupid. Why couldn't she figure this out?

Never before had she struggled with so many questions. Her aunt's and uncle's answers failed to satisfy her. She was determined to get a tighter grasp on what life was all about. And she would do it before she went back to Wisconsin.

CHAPTER NINE

The Boat or the Shore?

"Hurry, Uncle Bob! The phone is ringing!" Christy stood by the locked front door of the beach house with her arms full while her uncle lifted suitcases from the Mercedes' trunk. Aunt Marti was still in the car, checking her hair in the mirror. "Hurry, hurry!" Christy cried.

But, of course, by the time he dashed over and stuck the key in the door, the phone had stopped.

"I'll check the answering machine," Christy offered as Bob returned to unload the car.

She listened carefully to the messages of the past three days and saved all of them. None of the calls were from Todd. With slow, dragging steps, Christy trudged upstairs to her room. Why didn't he call? Was it because he knew she was out of town?

Bob pushed the door open with her suitcase. "Oh, sorry! I didn't realize you were in here."

"That's okay. Could you lift it up on the bed for me?"

The first thing Christy took out was the bag with the sweat-shirt in it. As she held Todd's up, a flood of second thoughts engulfed her. Would he think it was dumb? Should she really give it to him? Maybe it would be all right if she waited for the right moment—like when he came over to see her, or when he came to pick her up for their next date, or . . .

"Mail call!" Uncle Bob hollered just outside Christy's door.

Her heart jumped with farfetched hope. What if Todd had sent her a card! One of those cute, sweet, but not-too-mushy ones. She grabbed the four envelopes and quickly scanned the return addresses. One from her mom, one from Paula, no, two from Paula, and one from her little brother. Oh, well. So much for dreams.

"Don't get too excited, now," Uncle Bob teased, watching disappointment overtake her.

Christy blushed, surprised that her thoughts showed so transparently on her face. She opened one of the letters from Paula first, and a $10 bill floated to the floor.

"Money, money, money!" Uncle Bob sang out. "Boy, sure wish I got mail like that! What kind of sweepstakes did you win?"

Christy scanned the letter. "It's from Paula. See, we had this contest, and I kind of won. Sort of."

"I see." He raised his eyebrow speculatively.

"Well, I did win, really, but I guess I just don't feel like I thought I would. Oh, never mind."

"So, here you two are." Aunt Marti joined them.

"Hey, listen to this." Christy read the letter from her eight-year-old brother, David.

Dear Christy,

I miss you. I hope you are having a nice time at Uncle Bob and Aunt Martha's house. I hope you have fun when you go to Disneyland. Don't forget to buy something for me at Disneyland. I want a hat. Have fun.

Love,
David Miller

"Isn't that cute? 'David Miller.' Like I don't know his last name. Too bad he's not that cute in real life." Christy stuffed the letter back into the envelope. "When are we going to Disneyland, anyway? Sure would be fun to go on my birthday, which is only a few weeks away, hint, hint!"

Aunt Marti looked to Bob for an answer. He didn't say anything, so she spoke up. "I'm not exactly a Disneyland kind of person. That's more in your uncle's line of activities. You'll take her for her birthday, won't you, dear?"

Uncle Bob smiled one of his sly grins and said, "I don't think I'm exactly the guy Christy wants to go to Disneyland with, if she had her choice."

Uncle Bob winked, Christy blushed, and Aunt Marti suddenly caught on.

"Oh!" she exclaimed. "I imagine you'd like to have Todd take you on your birthday! Wouldn't that be marvelous? Well, you just never can tell what might happen between now and July 27th. Think positively, Christy! Your dreams can come true." Aunt Marti swished out of the room, leaving the fragrance of her perfume behind her.

Christy read her other two letters. Things at home hadn't changed much. Paula sounded the same. Her mother sounded the same. How could they stay the same when so much had changed for her? She lifted her new blue dress from the suitcase and held it up, studying her reflection in the mirror. Hardly seemed like the same girl who had cried over her image in this mirror a few weeks ago.

Her short hair now fell into its own natural wave, and although it wasn't as stunning as when Maurice had fixed it, it still looked pretty on her. At this very moment, she didn't regret having it cut. Her sunburned shoulders had peeled, but her face had stayed tanned and freckled, giving her a sporty appearance. She liked how she looked. And now she had this gorgeous little blue dress that Uncle Bob said made her eyes light up like "two limpid pools," whatever that meant.

Marti was the one who had an eye for clothes. She had picked this outfit, complete with new shoes, with special care at the Macy's across from their hotel. At Ghirardelli Square, they found silver earrings that were dangly and daring. It was the kind of outfit that should be worn someplace special. Like maybe on a date? With Todd? All she could do was hope.

Christy was anxious to get down to the beach the next day. Anxious to see if Todd would be there, anxious to see if he would ask her out. She was so anxious that she was out on the beach before anyone else that morning. Almost anyone else. One person sat in a beach chair near the shore: Alissa.

All kinds of mixed feelings swarmed over Christy. Alissa hadn't gone to Shawn's funeral. She might not even know. Christy considered turning around and running in the other direction, but Alissa had already seen her and was waving for her to come over.

"The weather is perfect today!" Alissa greeted Christy, acting genuinely glad to see her.

"Hi," Christy responded. "How was your date at the party last week?" What she really wanted to say was, "Why did you leave me, you traitor! Why are you so perfect and so horrible at the same time?"

"Wonderful!" Alissa bubbled. "His name is Erik, and he drives a Porsche, and we've been together every day since the party. This is the first time I've been down to the beach in almost a week."

"Alissa," Christy said cautiously. "Did you hear about Shawn?"

"Hear what?"

Christy gulped. "He went bodysurfing off the jetty the night of the party. Well, during the party, actually, but after you left with Erik."

"So?"

"So, I don't know how to tell you, but he crashed into the jetty and they took him to the hospital."

"Probably serves him right," Alissa said, pouring coconut-scented suntan oil on her long legs.

"Alissa, he didn't make it. He died."

Alissa's jaw twitched slightly. Christy couldn't read her expression under her sunglasses.

"Shawn's dead," Christy said in barely a whisper.

"That's too bad," Alissa remarked, looking out at the ocean. "Did I tell you that Erik has a Porsche? It's black with black interior."

Christy couldn't believe her ears. "Alissa! I just told you Shawn died, and all you can talk about is a dumb car? Didn't you hear what I said?"

"Yes, I heard you."

"Aren't you shocked or anything?"

"Listen." Alissa flipped off her sunglasses. Her eyes bore into Christy's. "Maybe you're too young to know what life is all about, so let me tell you. Life is hard, little girl, and the sooner you figure that out, the better off you'll be."

Christy pulled back as Alissa continued her venomous speech. "Shawn died, okay? He's dead. People die, you know. They leave you, and you can't get all depressed about it. They're gone. There's nothing you can do to change that. You've got your life to live, so do what you want and let everybody else burn. If you want any happiness, you have to make your own, because when it's over, it's over."

"But—" Christy began.

"But nothing, girl!" Alissa interrupted. Her face burned fiery red, but her eyes remained like ice. "You're on your own. Nobody is out there waiting to answer your prayers or make your dreams come true!"

Christy released her breath and tried to think of something to say, but nothing came to her.

Alissa lay down on her towel with her eyes closed and her face toward the sun, dismissing Christy now that her speech was over.

Christy wasn't sure what to do. Inwardly, she churned with anger. How could anyone be so cruel and coldhearted? The more she thought about it, the more she wanted to yell back at Alissa and tell her she was wrong. There *was* more to life than living it up and then dying! But that's as far as she could get in her mental argument. She couldn't refute any of the things Alissa said by offering a better solution.

Completely exasperated, Christy jumped up and headed for the water. She went in only ankle-deep, sloshing along the shoreline. After the water had cooled off her feet and time had cooled off her anger, she headed back to her towel. She had decided to face Alissa calmly, saying whatever came to her.

To her relief, Alissa was gone. Christy stretched out on her towel, letting the sun comfort her with its soothing rays. About half an hour later, someone came up beside her.

"Hey! How's it goin'?" It was Todd.

"Hi!" Christy quickly sat up. Seeing Todd left her at a loss for words. "Hi!" she said again.

"Do you want to go to a concert tonight?" Todd sure had a way of getting to the point.

"A concert?" Christy's heart raced. "Sure!"

"How was your trip?"

Christy tried to calm down and sound a bit more mature. "Good. We had a really good time."

Todd smiled his wonderful, wide smile. "Come on," he invited. "Let's go in the water."

For the next few hours, Christy felt more alive than she ever had before. The water sparkled like a field of diamonds in the midday sun, and the waves came at them gently and calmly.

At one point, when a bigger than usual wave surged above them, Todd grabbed her hand and yelled, "Dive under!" His touch seemed so strong, yet tender in a way that warmed Christy even in the cool water. He held on until they came up on the other side of the wave, and then he was the one who let go. Christy wanted to feel that surge of excitement from his touch again, and her mind played with how wonderful it would be to hold hands with him that night at the concert.

"I'm ready to go in," he said after some time. "How about you?"

"Sure. I'm ready for something to eat, too."

"I brought some pretzels," Todd offered back on the beach as they dried off.

"Good!" responded Christy. "All I've got is some sparkling mineral water my aunt stuck in my bag. But at least she gave me two bottles!"

As they munched pretzels, Christy told Todd all about her trip to San Francisco: riding the cable cars, tossing quarters into the guitar cases of street musicians, eating the best chocolate in the world at Ghirardelli Square, stuffing herself with crab at Alioto's. She even told him about the heated conversation about God that she had had with her aunt and uncle.

Todd listened attentively and then asked, "What did they say when you challenged them on their ideas about God?"

"The whole subject was dropped," Christy told him. "That's how it is with my aunt and uncle. They act like they have all the answers, but when I try to get something specific out of them, they change the subject."

"Yeah, my parents do the same thing," Todd said.

Two small boys chasing each other to the water ran across Todd's towel, kicking sand into the bag of pretzels.

"Oh well!" Todd said, grabbing the bag and peering inside. "Now we won't be able to tell if we're eating salt or sand on the pretzels." Todd tried to laugh at his own joke, but Christy thought his laugh seemed forced.

"Todd, how have you been doing since . . . ," Christy floundered, "since, you know, the funeral?"

"I haven't slept much. I keep thinking about that night over and over again, trying to figure out what I could have done to stop him."

"That must be awful for you."

"It is."

Christy looked around. The beach was full of people today, but she didn't see any of the other surfers.

"Todd?" Christy's voice was low, her tone direct. "I feel as though I have a lot of unanswered questions since Shawn died, and I think you're about the only one who might understand what I'm trying to figure out. Can I ask you some questions?"

"Sure."

"Okay," she began. "First, how do you know you're going to heaven when you die?"

"Because I accepted Christ last summer."

"But what does that mean—'accept Christ'? I mean, I accept Him—I accept that He's God's Son and all that. I've never rejected Him or anything."

Todd looked out at the ocean. He seemed to be thinking hard. "It's so simple that it's hard to explain," he finally said. "People have a free choice to either live life their own way or live it God's way."

"But what *is* God's way?" Christy practically shouted. "My

uncle keeps telling me to be true to myself, and Alissa was telling me that I've got to make my own way, and all my aunt does is avoid reality and try to think positively. I'm so mixed up!"

"I can see how you would be."

"At home it was easy. We all went to the same church, and everyone believed in God. Now you're telling me I have to live my life God's way if I want to go to heaven. What is God's way?"

Christy took her eyes off Todd and looked out at the ocean. She didn't like it when she came across so dumb.

"It's like this," Todd explained. "You're looking out at the Pacific Ocean, right? Somewhere out there is Hawaii. Imagine that Hawaii is heaven. You'd never make it there swimming all by yourself. You need a boat. Jesus is like that boat. Do you follow me?"

"Sort of."

"Well, it's up to us to make the choice. We can reject a free ride on the boat to Hawaii, or we can sit here and say, 'Yes, I believe in that boat, and I believe in Hawaii.' But unless we actually get on the boat, we're never going to make it to Hawaii." Todd seemed pretty pleased with his illustration, but Christy was only slightly less confused.

"I believe all that," Christy agreed. There seemed to be something deeper to what he was saying, but she just didn't get it.

"Yes," Todd challenged, "but have you turned your life over to Jesus? Or are you sitting on the shore saying, 'I believe in the boat, and I believe in Hawaii,' but you haven't actually gotten into the boat yet?"

Todd touched an area she wasn't quite ready to wrestle with. She pictured herself getting into a boat headed for Hawaii. It seemed risky—giving up the safety of being on shore, riding a boat through the wild waves.

"Oh well," she said and smiled at Todd. "That gives me something to think about. I'll let it settle in for a while. I need to get back to the house pretty soon."

"I'll pick you up for the concert at about 6:30?" Todd asked.

"Okay. I'll see you then!" Christy grabbed her stuff and headed for the house.

Life was really looking up. This was too good to be true! Christy thought about how she had accomplished so much by taking her aunt's advice. She really was becoming her own person.

"Aunt Marti!" she called, throwing open the screen door. "Uncle Bob!" She found them in the living room, looking at a book of wallpaper samples.

"Guess what! Todd asked me out for tonight! Can you believe it! A concert! And he's going to pick me up at 6:30! That means I only have three hours to get ready! I'd better get in the shower! I'm so excited!"

"Wonderful!" exclaimed Marti. "What are you going to wear, dear? Don't you think the new dress from San Francisco will be perfect?"

"I guess so. I hadn't really thought about what to wear. I'm just worried that my nose is starting to peel. Look at it."

"Haven't you been using the sunscreen I got you?" she scolded as the two of them headed up the stairs. Then turning to her husband, she added, "Robert, be a dear and call Maurice to cancel my nail appointment this afternoon. I need to help Christy get ready!"

Standing alone with the book of wallpaper, Uncle Bob called up the stairs to his two elated women: "Noooooo problem!"

CHAPTER TEN

Big Night Out

At 6:00 sharp, Uncle Bob placed the platter of grilled chicken, potatoes, and salad on the dining room table. Aunt Marti was finishing filling the crystal goblets with water when Christy appeared in the doorway, wearing her new blue dress with silver accessories.

"You look absolutely stunning, dear!" Aunt Marti praised. "Don't you think her hair turned out nicely, Bob?"

"You look beautiful, honey. You ought to knock this guy right off his feet!"

"Thanks," Christy said with a confident smile. "I really like this dress, Aunt Marti. Thank you for getting it for me."

"You know," Christy commented as they sat down to dinner, "people were actually dressed like this at that party I went to, and I felt so dumb wearing jeans! I'm glad to have something nice to wear tonight."

Aunt Marti smiled and looked pleased with herself.

"What concert are you going to?" Bob asked, offering Christy the platter of chicken.

"I don't know. But you don't have to worry about Todd. He's a great guy, and I'm sure he wouldn't take me to anything raunchy."

At 6:25 they all went into the living room to wait for the door-bell to ring. Christy carried in a gift-wrapped box and propped it by the front door.

"What's that?" Bob questioned.

"It's the sweatshirt I got Todd in San Francisco. Tonight should be a perfect time to give it to him. I hope he likes it!"

"He will, darling," Aunt Marti assured her. "He should be here any minute!"

They waited and waited. Finally, at 7:00 Uncle Bob started suggesting why Todd might be late.

"Maybe he stopped to get you flowers."

"Oh, Uncle Bob! Guys don't do that kind of thing anymore."

"Then maybe he chickened out!"

"Robert!" reprimanded Aunt Marti. "What a horrible thing to say!"

Tears filled Christy's eyes.

"Well," he defended, "I was only trying—"

Just then the doorbell rang. Christy blinked to keep her mas-cara from streaking. As she hurried to the door, she quickly grabbed the gift and concentrated on looking bright and cheerful. After all, Todd was bound to have some good reason for being so late.

Opening the door, she put on her sweetest smile and greeted Todd with an enthusiastic, "Hi there!"

Then she froze. He was wearing shorts! Shorts and a T-shirt! Why, oh why, had she worn a dress?

Todd didn't seem to notice that she was overdressed. Nor did he apologize for being half an hour late. His voice came out smooth and casual. "Hey, how's it going? You ready?"

Christy called out "Good-bye" over her shoulder and hurried to close the door before Aunt Marti could see what Todd had on. Too late. Bob and Marti had stepped into the entryway, and Bob was stretching out a hand to Todd.

"Good to see you, Todd. You remember my wife, Marti."

"Todd," Marti said with a smile, then calmly added, "so nice to see you again." She turned her back to him slightly and gave Christy a panicked look. "Are you sure you're ready to go, dear?"

Christy read the clue. She knew it was her opportunity to change clothes, but she really didn't know what to change into. She just wanted to leave with Todd. Now. Before anything could stop or change this opportunity.

"I think I'm all ready," Christy answered.

"You're sure, dear?" Marti gave her another piercing look.

"Yes, I'm sure. Let's go, Todd."

"Good night, then," Todd said to Marti. Turning to Bob, he added, "We'll be back before 11:00, sir."

"That's fine. Have a good time."

Christy and Todd headed toward the car.

"What's that?" Todd asked, looking at the box.

"I almost forgot! It's for you." Her voice came out shaky.

"For me? What is it?"

"Something I got you in San Francisco. If you don't like it, that's okay." Why had she bought him anything? Why was she dressed up? Why did she always feel so dumb? For a split second, she considered telling him she didn't feel well and couldn't go. But then they were at the door of his old Volkswagen van, which he affectionately called "Gus the Bus."

Todd slid the door open, and Christy nearly let out a scream. The van was full of people! And another girl was already sitting in the front passenger seat—Tracy!

Todd made quick introductions. "You know Tracy and Doug. This is Brian, Heather, Leslie, and Michelle."

The only open seat was way in the back of the van. Christy retreated to the seat as fast as she could, her face hot with anger and embarrassment. And what was worst of all was that everyone had on jeans! She felt ridiculous in her fancy outfit. What were all these other people doing here, anyway? Hadn't Todd asked her for a date? What was Tracy doing here? Christy felt sick to her stomach.

"What's that?" Doug asked as Todd pulled out of the driveway.

"Something Christy got me in San Francisco."

"Here, I'll open it!" Tracy offered from the passenger seat.

Before Todd could answer, she tore off the wrapping and held the sweatshirt up so everyone in the van could see. The remarks stung like saltwater. "Just what you need, Todd!" and "Guess she figured you out, convict!"

Christy didn't say a word all the way to the concert. Everyone else talked and laughed but didn't include her. They pulled into the parking lot of what looked like a community center, and the gang headed for the front door, where a crowd funneled its way into the auditorium.

"Come on!" Tracy called, pulling at Todd's arm. "If we hurry we can still get seats near the front!"

The others whooshed off with Tracy, but Christy lagged behind, desperately wishing that Todd would notice and come back to walk with her or at least pay some attention to her. But he didn't.

The fantasy balloon she had filled all afternoon completely deflated as she entered the large auditorium and sank down into a seat between Michelle and Heather. Tracy positioned herself between Todd and Doug at the end of the aisle and leaned forward to give a cute little wave to Michelle.

"That's it!" Christy growled under her breath. "I'm leaving."

"Did you say something?" Michelle asked.

"I'm not feeling real great," Christy said, startled that

Michelle had heard her and even more startled that she talked to her. "I think I'll go call my uncle and ask him to come get me."

"You can't go now!" Michelle said. "The concert is ready to start. You won't want to miss it."

Just then the lights dimmed, and a young man walked onto the stage to announce the performer.

Michelle turned to Christy and asked enthusiastically, "Do you have any of her CD's?"

"Who?" Christy shouted over the clapping as everyone else rose to their feet.

"Debbie Stevens," Michelle hollered and pointed to the energetic, young performer who appeared on stage, dazzling the crowd with her vibrant appearance.

"No! This is the first time I've heard her," Christy answered, stunned by the loud music and the crowd's excitement.

Clear and strong, Debbie's energetic voice filled the auditorium:

> Everyone is telling me
> Which way I should go,
> But no one has the answers.
> Don't you know?
> I'm no fool. I look at you.
> You're not living what you say.
> Can anybody show me?
> There's got to be a better way.

Christy listened carefully to the words. Surprisingly, she could understand most of them as the music loosened the self-pity knots that had tightened around her throat and stomach. Out of the corner of her eye, she could see Tracy swaying and clapping with the beat, laughing and moving free as a breeze. Todd and Doug followed Tracy's lead, and when Debbie announced the next song, they whistled and clapped with their arms over their heads.

Great! This is everybody's favorite song, and I've never heard it, Christy thought.

> You won't find it at the mall.
> It never goes on sale.
> You can't put it on your credit card
> Or order through the mail.
> Its value is priceless,
> But for you, today, it's free.
> Just give your heart to Jesus
> And get life eternally.
> You can't buy it,
> The price already's been paid.
> Jesus bought it for ya
> When He raised up from the grave.

"Is this a religious kind of concert?" Christy asked Michelle.

"Yes!" said Michelle. "This is the church we all go to."

"This is a church?" Christy scanned the large room. It looked like any huge, windowed auditorium. The only hint that it might be a church was the long, padded benches they sat on.

As the concert continued, Christy listened with a discerning ear. The songs all had hidden messages, she realized, and since this was the kind of thing Todd liked, she wanted to try to get into it, too. Maybe he would be more interested in her if she could talk to him about "the Lord" the way Tracy did.

She looked down the aisle at Todd. *He's so cute!* she thought. *I wish he liked me!*

Debbie sang for nearly 40 minutes before introducing her final song. She asked everyone to sit down. "I want to tell you a story about something that happened to me a few years ago."

The group respectfully quieted down.

"I came to this same auditorium four summers ago with some friends and listened to a band play. At the end, the drummer talked about how he had surrendered his life to Jesus and that he and all the other guys in the band were now Christians."

Debbie walked to the edge of the stage and continued to talk while she gestured with her hands. As she spoke in her animated fashion, she shook her head, causing the little curls around her face to shiver. "I couldn't figure out what they were talking about, because I grew up in a family that went to church all the time, and I thought I automatically was a Christian."

Debbie's words penetrated Christy.

"Then the lead singer told how to become a Christian, and a lot of people prayed with him that day. But I didn't. I didn't see why I needed to ask forgiveness for my sins. I mean, I was a pretty good person. I hadn't killed anybody, I never cheated on tests, and I tried to obey my parents. I didn't see what Jesus needed to 'save' me from, like these guys were talking about."

Christy glanced down the aisle, and Todd caught her gaze and smiled back. Her cheeks warmed as she focused back on the stage.

"Well," Debbie continued, "the next evening I rode my bike down to the beach and sat on a bench for a long time, just thinking. One of the guys had quoted a verse from the Bible that went like this: 'For all have sinned and fall short of the glory of God.'

"As I sat there, looking out at the roaring ocean and watching the sky turn all the colors of a rose garden, I realized I had come short of the glory of God. It suddenly became so clear! No matter how good I tried to be or how many self-improvement plans I tried, I could never be good enough to stand before God, because He is perfect and holy. I needed Jesus to open a way for me to get to God.

"Right then and there I prayed a prayer that went something

like this: 'Lord Jesus, I need You. Please forgive my sins and come into my life. Make me the woman You want me to be. Amen.'

"This next song I'm going to sing," Debbie said, "is one I wrote that night when I returned from my bike ride. That was probably one of the happiest nights of my life, because even though for so long I didn't think I needed Jesus, He knew I needed Him, and He never gave up on me."

The music began soft and slow, and Debbie sang,

> I didn't think I needed You in my life
> Until today.
> When in Your very special way
> You showed me
> How You wanted me,
> Showed me how You cared for me
> Even when I didn't care.
> Now I surrender my life to You
> Give You all of my heart
> You're the one I've waited for
> Even though I didn't know.
> Oh, Lord,
> It was You who loved me first.

"What a pretty song," Christy whispered to Michelle.

Debbie closed her eyes and held the microphone close to her mouth as she repeated the final line, "Oh, Lord, it was You who loved me first."

The auditorium fell completely still. As the last strains of music faded, Debbie opened her eyes and in a gentle voice said, "If you haven't yet surrendered your life to Jesus, I'm praying you will tonight. He's there waiting. Lord bless you! Thanks for coming!"

The houselights came on, and people started chattering as

they moved down the aisles to the back doors. Todd's group stuck together in their row, waiting for the crowd to subside.

"Hey, you guys! Let's try to go backstage and meet Debbie!" Doug suggested.

"Yeah, right!" said Heather.

"Come on!" he urged, leading the group up to the stage and looking for a way to get to the back.

"Can I help you guys?" asked one of Debbie's band members.

"We want to meet Debbie," Doug said confidently. "Do you think she would have time for some fans?"

"Sure, I don't see why not," the guy said. "Follow me."

He led them to a side door and down a short hallway to a small room, where he knocked on the door and said, "Debbie? You've got some fans here who want to meet you."

Debbie opened the door wide and blurted out, "Hi, fans!" Then she immediately flushed a deep red and turned to the guy in the band, slugging him in the arm. "Mark!" she gasped. "I thought you were kidding! I didn't know anyone was really here!"

They all laughed, which helped everyone relax, and Debbie regained her composure, shaking hands with each of them and asking their names. When she came to Christy, she said, "I'm so glad you came tonight!"

"I am, too," Christy said.

"You know," Debbie told her, "I've always liked the name Christy. It means 'follower of Christ.' Did you know that?"

"No," Christy answered, surprised at Debbie's friendliness. Weren't singers supposed to be aloof, temperamental, and very protective of their backstage lives? Debbie sparkled with her genuineness.

"Your concert was awesome!" Doug said.

"I have all three of your CD's," Michelle said. "Do you have another one coming out soon?"

"Hopefully by December." Debbie flashed a bright smile.

Her shiny black hair curled in little ringlets across her forehead, and Christy thought she looked quite pretty. It wasn't necessarily her makeup, because she didn't have much on. But there was something about the way her eyes glistened that made her beautiful.

"I really liked your last song," Christy told her rather shyly. "It made me feel something."

"Oh? What did you feel?" Debbie asked.

"It's hard to explain." Christy wished everyone wasn't standing there, staring at her.

Todd may have sensed her uneasiness because he cut in and said, "We want to go buy some of your CD's, Debbie. Do you have a table at the back?"

"Yes," Debbie said.

Tracy piped up, "Will you autograph them for us?"

"Sure," Debbie said. Then reaching over and touching Christy on the arm, she said, "Do you want to stay here and visit for another minute?"

"Me?" She didn't really, but she felt put on the spot and didn't know how to say no.

"We'll be back in just a minute," Todd told her and followed Tracy and the others out the door.

"So, tell me. What did my song make you feel?" Debbie asked, offering Christy a chair.

It took Christy a few seconds to clear her thoughts. Here she was, alone with a complete stranger who was asking her about her innermost feelings. All she could think of was that Todd probably wanted to get rid of her so he could put his arm around Tracy or something. What if they left without her?

"I . . . I don't remember," Christy stammered.

"That's okay," Debbie assured her. "I didn't mean to make

you feel uncomfortable. I like talking to people after concerts to see how the Lord spoke to them through the music."

"Well, I really just came with some of my friends who come to a lot of these concerts. Maybe you should ask one of them because they talk about the Lord all the time."

"Can I ask you something?" Debbie's eyes flashed their sparkles.

"I guess so."

"Christy, if you were to die tonight, do you know for certain that you would go to heaven?"

Christy's heart pounded. She had gone over and over that question when Shawn died. She had challenged her aunt and uncle on it, but nobody had ever asked her. "I'm pretty sure I would."

"There's a way you can be absolutely sure," Debbie said. "By asking Jesus to forgive your sins and come into your heart."

Why did they leave me here for Debbie to pin me down like this? Christy's heart raced.

"Yes, I know all that," she told Debbie. "I've gone to church since I was a baby."

"That's good," Debbie said. "But it's not enough. See, everyone has sinned, which makes us unable to come before God, who is holy. The penalty for sin is death, and that's why Jesus died. To pay the price for our sins. Only through Jesus can we be saved."

Why is she preaching at me like this? Christy thought, feeling more and more angry at the group for leaving her.

"Thanks for your time," Christy said, trying to be polite. "But I'd really better go try to find my friends before they leave without me."

"Okay. Here," Debbie offered, "I'd like to give you one of my CD's. Everything I've been saying is in the words of the songs." She handed Christy a CD from out of a gym bag on the floor. Her

THE CHRISTY MILLER SERIES

photo and the words, "Be Real," were printed on the front.

"Thanks," Christy mumbled. Then, feeling she had been rude to cut her off so fast, she told Debbie, "I'll listen to it. I promise I will."

Debbie touched Christy's shoulder and looked gently into her eyes. "Just promise you'll listen to the Lord when He speaks to your heart."

Christy looked away. "Okay. Thank you again. This is really nice of you. I'd better go. Thanks."

The ride home proved to be as exasperating as the ride to the concert. Todd asked if anyone wanted to get something to eat.

"Sure!" exclaimed Tracy. "As long as we don't go to Hanson's Parlor!" She suggested they go to her house, because her mom had made cookies that afternoon, and unless her three brothers had gotten to them, plenty should be left.

The last thing Christy felt like doing was spending another hour or so around Tracy, on her territory.

"I think I'd better go home," Christy piped up from her back-seat prison, adding, "if that's okay with you, Todd." She hoped he would object and beg her to come along.

"Sure, if that's what you want."

Why did he have to be so easygoing and agreeable all the time?

"Your house is on the way to Tracy's anyhow," he added.

To Christy's surprise, instead of just dropping her off at the curb, Todd got out and walked her to the door.

"I'm glad you came tonight," he told her as they stood under the front light.

"You are? I didn't think you even noticed I was there with all your other friends."

Todd gave her a puzzled look. "Of course I noticed you. I hope you can come with us again sometime. When do you go back to Wisconsin?"

"The end of August. I don't remember the exact day."

"Well, good night," he said, giving her a quick hug. His tanned face was only inches from hers. "See you tomorrow?"

"Okay!" Her heart melted. "See you!"

How could Todd do this to her? Up and down. Up and down. Did he have any idea what an emotional roller coaster he kept sending her on? She watched him walk to the van and gave a half-hearted wave to the others waiting for him.

"Hey," Todd called from the sidewalk, "I like your dress!" Then he sprinted to the driver's side, and with a pop and sputter, Gus the Bus chugged down the street.

Bob and Marti were in the den. Uncle Bob was watching TV with the sound turned down, and Marti was talking on the phone. She hung up immediately, anxious to hear all about the big date.

Christy gave a brief rundown of the disappointing evening, leaving out the part about it being a Christian concert. She did tell them how everyone went to Tracy's house, but how she had no desire to go.

"Why, that horrid girl!" Marti exclaimed. "How dare she weasel in on your boyfriend like that!"

"She's really not horrid," Christy admitted, "and Todd isn't exactly my boyfriend. I mean, he obviously invited her to the concert, too! He invited all of them. But," Christy added with a smile, "he did like my dress, and he did say he would see me tomorrow."

"That's my man!" said Uncle Bob, his eyes still fixed on the television. "Give him time. He'll come around."

"That's the problem!" Christy wailed. "I haven't got a whole lot of time. I'm going home in a few weeks!"

"Hang in there. Hang in there!" Bob muttered.

"How am I supposed to hang in there?" Christy asked, trying to get him to take his eyes off the TV and look at her. "How do I get him to like me?"

"Slam him! That's the way! Down on the floor! Now's your chance! Go for it!"

Christy glared at her uncle and then at the TV. "Wrestling!" she squawked. "I'm asking you for advice, and I think you're listening, but you're talking to some fake wrestler in a cape and mask!"

"Oh, Robert!" scolded Aunt Marti.

"What?" He looked up, startled. "Did you say something?"

"Men!" sputtered Christy. "You're all weird! Weird! Weird! Weird!"

CHAPTER ELEVEN

Everything a Girl Could Ever Want

Christy walked the four blocks to Alissa's house slowly. An hour earlier Alissa had called, asking Christy to come over. She had reluctantly agreed, but the closer she got to Alissa's house, the more timid and uncertain she felt.

Alissa had sounded upset on the phone, and Aunt Marti said she had called the night before while Christy was at the concert. What did she want? And why had she called Christy instead of Erik?

Alissa answered the door with her usually perfect hair covering her right eye. Her shirt and shorts were wrinkled. "Come on in," she offered in an emotionless voice and showed Christy to the living room. They stepped around half-packed suitcases, and Alissa lifted a box off the couch so they could sit down.

"Are you leaving already?" Christy asked. "I thought your family was staying till the end of August."

"We were, but now we're not," Alissa replied softly. "I'm leaving to go back to my grandmother's in Boston."

"What about the rest of your family?"

"The rest of my family?" Alissa laughed. "What about the rest of my family?" Her eyes flashed their familiar fury. "I'll tell you about the rest of my family! This is it—me! That's my family."

"What do you mean?" Christy feared that Alissa might go into one of her rages, but she saw something different on Alissa's face that caused her to pity her.

"It's like this. I'm an only child, and my dad died three months ago of lung cancer," Alissa stated, the anger subsiding.

"Oh, I'm sorry. I didn't know," Christy said.

"I didn't tell you. So, my mom and I came here to rest and regroup for the summer. Except my mom brought an old friend with her. Her bottle."

"What do you mean?"

"I mean," Alissa squeezed out, "my mom is an alcoholic. She supposedly got help from a treatment center a few years ago, but as soon as my dad died, she started to drink again. She stayed inside this house since the day we arrived and drank and drank until she didn't know where we were or how long we'd been here."

Alissa turned her head to look out the window, and Christy noticed her right eye was bruised and swollen. "How awful, Alissa! Are you okay? What happened to your eye?"

"My mom threw a punch at me when I tried to get her to go to bed last night. Erik was supposed to come pick me up, and my mom was lying on the living room floor. Erik hadn't met my mom, and I didn't want him to see her like that, so I tried to drag her to the bedroom. She got furious. She hit me and threw a bottle of vodka at me. She went crazy, screaming that she'd kill me. I got really scared and ran down the street to a pay phone. I called the police. They took my mom away. I'm pretty sure they'll put her back in a rehabilitation center of some sort."

"That's terrible! Is there anything I can do?"

Alissa switched back to her cool, matter-of-fact self and said,

"I was hoping you could help me pack this stuff. I didn't know who else to ask. I've got so many phone calls to make, I'll never get this all done before my plane takes off at 4:00."

For the next hour, Christy numbly packed Alissa's abundant wardrobe. Her clothes were in three different closets. She had many gorgeous outfits, expensive jeans, and more shoes than Christy could count. Alissa finished her phone calls while Christy jammed cosmetics into a small suitcase for her. Opening the last drawer, she pulled out a handful of eyeliners, a mirror, and a round, plastic compact.

Wonder what this is? Christy thought, popping the top open. A circle of little white pills curved around the inside with a number underneath each one.

"Everything is set," Alissa said, walking into the bedroom. "My mom sobered up this morning and agreed to sign her admission papers. If all goes well with the program, they'll let her come back to Boston at the end of September. I packed her stuff this morning so I could drop it by the hospital on my way to the airport."

"How are you getting to the airport?"

"Erik said he'd take me."

"You're so lucky to have him," Christy said. "He must really love you. It's going to be awful leaving him, isn't it?"

"Oh! Where did you find those?" Alissa reached for the pink compact. "I've been looking for those for days."

The doorbell rang before Christy could respond.

"That's probably Erik," Alissa said, leaving Christy in the bedroom while she answered the door.

Christy heard Erik's voice echo down the hall, "You know I'm going to miss you."

Christy sat on the bed, thinking, *How sweet! I wonder if Todd will say anything like that to me when I go back home?*

"I'm glad you came, Erik." Alissa's voice was soft. "I'm not sure what I would have done if you hadn't come."

"I even came early," he pointed out. "Did you notice?"

"I'm glad, because I've got to take my mom her stuff."

"That shouldn't take too long." Erik's voice got lower. "There's still enough time for you to tell me good-bye."

"Stop it, Erik! Not now! I mean it!" Alissa's voice became muffled, and all Christy could hear were footsteps in the hall, coming toward the bedroom.

"Somebody is—" Alissa's voice came from the other side of the door.

Before she could finish the sentence, the bedroom door swung open. Christy jumped to her feet, her eyes wide. There stood Erik with his arm around Alissa. Christy panicked! What should she do?

"Hey!" he shouted. "What are you doing here?"

"I-I was just leaving!" Christy stammered.

"Don't bother!" Erik yelled, stomping down the hall.

"Erik!" Alissa cried, stumbling after him. "I need you! Don't go now!"

He yanked open the front door and shouted, "Hey! I needed you, too, but you didn't give a rip about me! I'm sick of your excuses and your little crybaby games. Grow up!"

He slammed the door, and Christy could hear his Porsche screech out of the driveway. She waited in the bedroom, not sure what to do next. Slowly, she made her way down the hall.

"Alissa?" she called. "Are you okay?"

"What a jerk! I never liked him anyway." Alissa's eyes brimmed with tears as Christy sat down beside her on the couch.

"I'm sorry I messed things up for you."

"It wasn't you." Alissa let the tears flow. "He's just a big baby who can't handle it when he doesn't get his way. I've got better things to do than waste my time on him!"

Apparently, she hadn't convinced herself. She buried her face in her hands and cried until the tears ran down her arms.

"It's okay." Christy looked around for some tissue. "You're going to be okay. You've got everything any girl could ever want."

Alissa lifted icy, bloodshot eyes to meet Christy's gaze. "Everything any girl could ever want?" she asked sarcastically. "Then why am I so lonely all the time, Miss Know-it-all? Can you tell me that? And why am I so miserable that . . ." She hesitated and then blurted out, ". . . that I tried to kill myself last December?" Her voice rose. "Can you answer me that?"

"No. I mean, I don't know." Christy felt the tears coming to her own eyes. "I can't believe you're telling me this, Alissa! You have everything. You're everything I want to be."

"No I'm not." Alissa dried her eyes and smoothed her long blond hair. "You just don't realize how good you have it. Stay innocent, Christy. Stay innocent."

For a moment, they both were silent. Christy ached inside; she desperately wanted to help Alissa, to offer her some answers. If only there were some way she could help her. Then she had an idea.

"Let me call my uncle and ask him to take you to the airport, okay?" It wasn't much, but she knew it was a start.

While they waited for Bob to arrive, Alissa pulled herself together and appeared to have recovered from the blowout with Erik. Within 20 minutes, Uncle Bob pulled into the driveway and loaded the car with Alissa's belongings. They stopped at the hospital, and Christy waited while Uncle Bob helped Alissa take her mother's suitcases inside.

During the trip to the airport, Christy wondered how much she should try to explain to Uncle Bob. But he rolled through the afternoon with graciousness, and it wasn't until the two of them were driving home that he asked Christy if there was anything she wanted to talk about.

"Men are weird," Christy said. "I can't believe the way Erik treated Alissa, and the way he walked out of her life as though he didn't care anything about her."

"I imagine Alissa has had lots of boyfriends like Erik," Bob contemplated. "She seems like a girl who has been around. That's not the best way to be."

"I'm beginning to see that. When I first met her, I thought she was perfect. I wanted to be just like her in every way. I couldn't believe it this morning when she said she was so miserable. Thanks for coming when I called you and helping her out. That's the second time this summer you've been there for me when my new friends were in trouble. Thanks."

"Anytime. You want to stop somewhere for dinner?"

"Sure. I'm starved," Christy replied. "Just as long as it isn't Hanson's Parlor."

"What?"

"Never mind. That's another problem I've got to work on."

CHAPTER TWELVE

Hopes and Heartaches

"Christy? Bob? Are you home?" Aunt Marti called from her bedroom. It was after 10:00, and they were just returning from dinner after taking Alissa to the airport.

"Yes, my little peach fuzz," Bob called up the stairs.

Marti hopped down the stairs in a long, floral-print silk robe. "Christy, I've the most marvelous news to tell you! Your boyfriend came by while you were gone and asked why you weren't at the beach today." She settled herself on the couch and continued. "I told him you were over at Alissa's, goofing off."

Christy shook her head. "We weren't exactly goofing off!"

"No matter," Marti continued. "Todd and I had a nice little chat, and he said he would call you this evening. Well, the poor guy has called twice, and I guess he gave up because he said he would talk to you tomorrow. He certainly is a charming young man, Christy."

"If only he thought I was a charming young woman!"

"Oh! I nearly forgot! It was the most darling thing you've ever seen. He was wearing the sweatshirt we got for him in San Francisco. It looked so adorable on him!"

"Was he really? I can't believe it!"

"That's my man," said Uncle Bob with a twinkle in his eye.

"Give him time. He'll come around."

"You flake!" Christy yelled and bopped him on the head with a pillow from the couch before heading up to her room. She decided to start a letter to Paula after getting ready for bed, but she kept falling asleep. Finally, she gave in to the exhaustion and crawled between the covers with a yawn.

The next morning, she lingered in bed for more than an hour finishing the letter to Paula and writing a short note to her parents. She probably would have stayed between the covers and dozed off again if she weren't so anxious to see Todd.

Should I go down to the beach or will he come by again? I think I'll wait—at least till noon, and then, if he doesn't call or come over, I'll go down to the beach.

With special care, Christy showered, did her hair, and put on her makeup, thinking of Alissa the whole time.

I wonder how Alissa is doing at her grandmother's? I hope things turn out better for her. I can't believe Erik dropped her like that. I thought he really liked her. I thought she had her life so together.

Pushing thoughts of Alissa from her mind, Christy surveyed her wardrobe. She had some new clothes she hadn't worn yet. But the longer she looked, the more discouraged she became. Nothing seemed right for today.

"I don't have anything to wear!" she moaned, flopping onto the bed. "Guess I'll wear my bathing suit, a pair of shorts, and a T-shirt again. I sure am getting tired of wearing the same thing all the time."

"Christy?" The tap of acrylic nails had become familiar. "Christy darling!"

"Come on in, Aunt Marti."

"Who were you talking to, dear?"

"Myself."

"You're still in your nightshirt!"

"Yeah. I can't find anything to wear," Christy sighed.

"Maybe we should go shopping again. But not this morning. I've got a meeting. Why don't we go later this afternoon, to South Coast Plaza? Bob could meet us there for dinner. Besides, I did want to find something for your birthday outing to—" She caught herself. "Well, to wherever you might go for your birthday."

"What are you trying to tell me, Aunt Marti?"

With a forced little laugh, she responded, "Absolutely nothing, dear. I simply thought it would be nice to do some birthday shopping for you." Marti glanced at her watch. "Oh dear! I really must be going. I'll be home around 2:30, and we can leave soon after that."

She turned her head back toward Christy and said, "You really should hurry and get dressed. It's not polite to keep him waiting."

"Keep who waiting?"

Marti gave her a puzzled look. "You mean I didn't tell you?" She tilted her head back and laughed at a joke only she was in on. "Oh, dear me! Where is my mind today? I came up to tell you that Todd is waiting in the den."

"He is?" Christy suppressed a shriek. "Why didn't you tell me? What am I going to wear?"

"I must go, dear! You have a good time today, and I'll see you around 2:30." She walked out the door, shaking her head and chuckling to herself.

Christy called out after her, "Tell him I'll be right down!" She scrambled to pull on a pair of shorts and a shirt and gave herself a quick glance in the mirror before bounding down the stairs.

"Hi, Todd! I'm sorry I left you waiting so long. My aunt didn't tell me you were here. I mean, she told me, but not right away. Otherwise, I wouldn't have left you here so long by yourself."

"It's all right. Do you want to go to Disneyland?" Todd sure had a way with words.

"You mean now?" Christy almost squealed.

"No. Next Friday. For your birthday."

"Are you kidding? Yes! How fun! I'd love to go!" Then Christy paused, her enthusiasm visibly diminishing.

"Who else is going?"

"Just you and me," Todd said. "Unless you want to take somebody else. It's your birthday."

Christy blushed, ashamed for thinking Todd planned to take another "Gus the Bus" full of people to Disneyland with them. This was special. Her birthday. He must have thought of that.

"No," she replied softy, "I don't want to invite anyone else. Unless you do."

"Nope. We can celebrate our birthdays together. You'll be 15, and I'll be one year old in the Lord."

"What?" Christy asked.

"Remember that night on the beach after Shawn's party? I told you I became a Christian last summer on July 27th, and that's when you told me that's your birthday. So, you'll be 15, and I'll be one."

Todd stuck out his square jaw and casually folded his arms across his chest. Christy thought he looked a little bit like Uncle Bob when he was about to tease her.

"Are you hungry or anything?" Christy asked. "I haven't eaten breakfast yet, and I think my uncle is still in the kitchen. Maybe we can get something to eat."

They found Bob in his usual chair at the kitchen table, dunking a donut into a cup of fresh coffee.

"Morning!" he greeted them. "You kids want some donuts?"

"Where did these come from?" Christy asked.

"When your aunt went out this morning, she told me I

needed some exercise. So, I briskly walked right down to the donut shop!" He winked at Christy. "I could use some help destroying the evidence, if you know what I mean."

Todd and Christy laughed and both pulled up chairs.

"What's the plan for today?" Bob asked.

"Marti and I are supposed to go to South Coast Plaza around 2:30. You're supposed to meet us there for dinner."

"Good thing I asked you. My 'social director' hadn't filled me in on the plans for the evening yet. Must have just been one of those things that slipped her mind," he said good-naturedly.

"Right," Christy agreed, remembering the incident in her room that morning. "Her mind has been slipping a bit lately."

"You know, it's only 11:00 now. If you two want something to do, you could take the tandem out for a spin. We bought that bike last summer, thinking we would get some exercise, but we've only used it twice."

"That would be fun! You want to, Todd?"

"Sure. Let's take it over to Balboa Island."

Bob helped them pull the bicycle from the garage and gave them a push into the street. Christy waved quickly and put her hand back on the handle bar to help steady the wobbly monster.

"I'm glad you're the one in front," Christy told Todd. "I'm not real coordinated on things like this."

Todd steered through the intersection; Christy did her best to keep her balance and not look at the cars roaring past them. They pedaled to the Balboa Island ferry. The ferry took on only a few cars at a time, but since they were the only ones with a bike, they got right on. Todd pulled out a handful of change and paid their fare. The ferry lurched forward, chugging loudly on its short trip to the island.

"Look at all the sailboats!" Christy exclaimed, moving closer to Todd.

"Now there's a hot catamaran," Todd said.

"Where?"

"See, over there." Todd pointed, and Christy moved closer so that her shoulder briefly pressed against his. She didn't know what a catamaran was, and she really didn't want to ask in case she sounded dumb. She just liked having an excuse to be close to Todd.

If only he would put his arm around me.

Before Todd could make a move, the ferry pulled into its dock, and they hopped on the bike. They rode up the narrow streets lined with little beach houses. Cottages, really. Christy liked all the stained-glass windows and bright flowers in the tiny front yards.

"Do you want a Balboa Bar?" Todd called over his shoulder.

"I've never had one!" Christy admitted.

They stopped at the ice cream stand, and Todd said, "You can't go to Balboa and not eat a Balboa Bar. What do you want on yours? Chips? Nuts? Sprinkles?"

Christy looked at the pictures of the varieties of the ice cream bar to choose from. People were waiting in line behind them, and the girl at the window peered at her impatiently.

"I don't know." She hated it when she lost all her confidence like this. She put the decision back on Todd. "I'll have whatever you do."

Todd ordered two of the chocolate-dipped ice cream bars with nuts. Christy hated nuts. But she didn't say anything.

They walked past the specialty boutiques along the main street, enjoying the treat. Christy tried to casually pick off the nuts as she ate her ice cream and barely paid attention to what they saw in the shop windows. Her mind felt bogged down with the frustration she had experienced a few minutes earlier.

Why do I have such a hard time making simple decisions? Why do

I always lose my confidence at key moments and act like a total idiot? Does Todd notice my insecurities? Does he like me? What about Tracy? Why is Tracy so much more self-confident and bubbly? Why can't I be more like her? Then a strange thought hit her. *How can I be true to myself like Uncle Bob keeps saying, when I really don't like who I am?* Christy realized she kept wanting to be like somebody else. First Alissa, now Tracy. And at home she had always imitated Paula. *Paula,* she thought. *If Paula could see me now! It's a good thing I didn't mail her letter yet. I've got lots more to tell her!*

"How do you like it?" Todd asked, indicating her ice cream bar.

"I like it," she said. Actually, she had eaten almost the whole thing and hadn't even noticed how it tasted. The sun was melting the chocolate, and she tried to lick the drips off the bar before they landed on her clothes. *What a jerk I've been. I've hardly talked at all. I hope Todd doesn't think I don't like him.*

"So," she began, realizing they had circled back to the bike, "what's new with you?"

"Not much," he said as they straddled the bike and pushed off. "What's new with you?" Then he smiled, and from the angle of his turned head, Christy thought she could see faint dimples in his bronzed skin. She hadn't noticed them before.

"This is fun," she said. "Thanks for coming." She leaned close to his broad shoulders so he could hear her.

"Sure," he replied, turning his head again. "We're going to ride the long way back, over the bridge instead of taking the ferry. Is that okay?"

"Sure." Christy leaned forward to check for his dimples. She wondered what it would be like to feel his cheek against hers. Her imagination sprinted. *What if Todd really starts to like me, and we start going together? Would he treat me the way Erik treated Alissa? What's going to happen in the weeks before I go home? Will I break my promise to my parents and end up doing something I'll regret later?*

Todd said something, but all she heard was the word "Tracy." She clenched her teeth and said, "What? I didn't hear what you said."

"I wondered if you knew what time it is. I told Tracy I would give her a ride home from work at 2:00."

Tracy! Why did he have to bring her up? Christy felt foolish for thinking about getting closer with Todd when he was far from having intimate thoughts about her. Christy pouted the rest of the bike ride home. Todd didn't seem to think anything of her silence.

When they got to the house, he helped her put the bike back in the garage. He smiled as if he were about to say something funny, but all he said was, "Later," and sprinted to Gus.

Christy watched Gus the Bus cruise down the street. As its faded tan backside disappeared through the intersection, she muttered, "Later."

Going through the back door of the house, Christy called out. Nobody was home. She scanned the refrigerator for something to eat and settled on a piece of barbecued chicken and a glass of milk.

For a long time she sat with her elbow on the kitchen table, her head resting in her palm. A familiar wave of depression came over her. Up and down. Down and up. Her whole life was a series of waves rushing in and pulling back. She wished she could some-how even out . . . find something stable to latch on to.

Having just spent the last two and a half hours with Todd, she should have been happy. Plus, she was going to Disneyland with him next week for her birthday. But she was miserable. All sum-mer she had gotten everything she wanted and more. More clothes than she could wear—and she was going shopping again this afternoon. More opportunities to go places and do things than she had ever had at home. She had been spoiled rotten by her aunt and uncle for weeks, but she just didn't feel happy, and she couldn't figure out why.

She glanced at the clock. A quarter till three, and Aunt Marti still wasn't home. Typical.

Christy wandered aimlessly through the house for a while, looking at all the expensive things that adorned it. *The buying never ends for my aunt*, she thought, and suddenly the words to the Debbie Stevens's song "You Can't Find It at the Mall" popped into her head. *Hmmm.* Christy was struck by a brief revelation. *Maybe Debbie was right. Maybe I do need Jesus in my life.* But that wasn't something she wanted to deal with at the moment. She needed to pull herself out of this emotional slump and thinking about Jesus Christ dying on the cross and about her being a sinner was certainly not going to cheer her up.

She meandered up the stairs, trying to decide what to change into when the front door burst open. "Christy dear! Are you ready to go?"

Christy snapped out of her fog and called down from the top of the stairs, "I'll be there in a second." She ran into her room and in record time changed into a denim skirt and one of the shirts she hadn't worn yet. She didn't even take time to look in the mirror, but galloped down the stairs calling, "I'm ready!"

Aunt Marti stood by the door with a stack of mail in her hand. She looked up at Christy and then frowned disapprovingly.

"What in the world is on your face, dear girl?"

"My face? I don't know."

Christy scurried to the downstairs bathroom with Aunt Marti on her heels. There, in the bathroom mirror, she saw it. A big glob of chocolate from the Balboa Bar had streaked across her cheek and dried, leaving a skid mark that stretched from her upper lip almost all the way to her ear!

Christy burst into tears. "No!" she sobbed. "No! No! No! Why am I such a klutz! Todd must have seen me like this; why didn't he say anything?"

Aunt Marti, apparently thinking Christy's outburst was overdone, scolded, "This is no way for a young lady to act. Calm yourself. Here I thought you were all ready to go shopping, but you haven't even washed your face. Now, go upstairs and do something about your eye makeup, too. And that shirt doesn't really go with that skirt, you know."

Christy stomped upstairs to redo herself according to Aunt Marti's directions, muttering and sniffing all the way.

Despite all the trauma, they actually made it to South Coast Plaza by 4:00. But Christy had a hard time getting into the mood to shop after all her aunt's reprimands.

"Christy, this is a cute skirt, don't you think?" her aunt said, holding up a short, green one.

"No. That shade of green isn't one of my colors, remember?" Christy jabbed. "But I like this." She held up a pleated plaid skirt. "This is perfect, don't you think?" It wasn't even that cute; but it was something Marti would never select.

After several encounters, Marti lowered herself into a chair and said with resignation, "It's up to you, Christy. Whatever you want. You know what you like."

Christy did something she had never done before. She went through the racks, randomly picking whatever appealed to her and tried it on. If it fit, she asked her aunt to buy it. She never looked at a price tag. Maybe the stack of new clothes would add up to more than $500. It was stupid, she knew, but it was the only way she could think of to get back at her aunt.

The total came to more than $700, but Aunt Marti put it all on her credit card without batting an eyelash. Suddenly, Christy felt sick to her stomach. Seven hundred dollars? She couldn't do it. She just couldn't do it. Besides, wasn't it Uncle Bob who really paid the bills?

"Wait," Christy said to the salesclerk. "I, um, I think I may have gotten some of the sizes wrong. Could you cancel that? I need to go try some of these on. I'd hate to get home and find out some things didn't fit."

Aunt Marti looked thoroughly annoyed. "Well, hurry along, dear. We're to meet your uncle in half an hour."

Christy slipped into the dressing room, the clerk following her with the stack of clothes. She peeled through the pile behind the closed door and settled on five items. They all sort of matched, and they were the things she liked best. One T-shirt was even on sale.

"Here." Christy handed the diminished stack to the clerk. "This is all."

"You're sure?" the clerk questioned.

"Yes."

Marti didn't say a word. She kept silent until they met Bob at the restaurant.

"Well, well!" he said, eyeing their bags. "Looks like you've met with some success."

"Yes," Marti said coolly. "If only your niece's taste in clothes were as strong as her impulsiveness, we would be doing quite well!"

Her comment hit Christy like a gale-force wind. That was it! Something snapped. In Christy's mind, Marti instantly transformed from a sophisticated, rich aunt to a snooty, self-centered peacock. So what if she had enough money to buy whatever she wanted? She didn't have much of a heart. Her lack of consideration for other people's time and feelings had showed itself over and over again.

Christy wanted to snap back: "I'm tired of you trying to make me into the perfect little daughter you never had. I don't need your money or your lectures anymore. I don't want to be the person you want me to be. I just want to be Christina Juliet Miller from Wisconsin. And if that's not good enough for you, then that's too bad." But all she said was, "I'd like to have steak for dinner. Is that okay with you, Uncle Bob?"

"Sure, honey. Whatever you would like."

Aunt Marti gave her a look of disdain and ordered the mini chef's salad.

Although Christy wasn't really hungry, she ate all her dinner, including a baked potato with gobs of butter and sour cream and a butterscotch sundae for dessert—just to prove to Marti that she was her own person. That night when she couldn't sleep because her stomach hurt, she wasn't sure exactly what she had proved.

The next few days Christy found more opportunities to silently rebel against her aunt's manipulations. They were subtle little things that she was sure Marti didn't even notice at first. But, for her, every act of insolence fanned the inner flame of dislike for her aunt.

One afternoon when she came in from the beach, she answered the phone and took a message for Marti about a special meeting at the community center that evening at 7:00. Christy purposely left the message hidden under the pad of paper until 6:30 that evening. Then she slyly put the note on top of the desk and said, "You did get the message by the phone, didn't you?"

It wasn't like her to be vengeful like this, but the more she held her frustrations inside, the more her bitter little darts flew. She had been around Marti enough to know what bothered her, and Christy purposefully did whatever she could to prompt the aggravation. Like eating in front of the TV, or leaving her sandy beach towel on her bedroom floor. Then there were the two killer pet peeves: slouching and nail biting. Christy did both, whenever possible, just to perturb her aunt.

Like a wounded animal, Marti backed off. Her aggressive attacks digressed into a timid routine of gentle reminders.

Coming in from the beach one afternoon, Christy met her aunt in the kitchen.

"A letter came for you," Marti said. "It's on your bed."

"Okay." Christy grabbed a handful of her uncle's secret recipe chocolate chip cookies and headed for her room.

"Say, Christy," her aunt called after her, "why don't you leave your towel here? I'll throw it in the wash for you. And perhaps you'd like to take a napkin with you. Just in case," she weakly added.

Christy stuffed a cookie into her mouth, ignoring the suggestions and fighting back the guilt she felt over acting like such a brat. She didn't like being this way, but once she started, it was easier to keep up the antics than to stop. She had never been good at apologizing. Especially when the other person deserved what she was getting.

Her room, bright and refreshing, looked tremendously inviting this afternoon. She found the letter on her bed, as Marti had said. To her surprise, she saw it was from Alissa. Christy read it over and over, realizing how good she really had it. Alissa's life sounded so sad and hopeless.

Dear Christy,

I arrived at my grandmother's with very few problems. I would like to thank you and your uncle for the ride to the airport and for your help in getting me packed.

My mother is keeping up with her alcohol control program, and the director of the center called yesterday to say that if she keeps improving, she will be released within a few weeks.

I'm staying with my grandmother until school starts, and then she is sending me to boarding school. My address is on the envelope.

It would be nice to hear from you if you have a chance to write.

I think about you and Todd and Shawn and Erik a lot. I regret how my time in Newport went, especially since it was so short. I know I said some cruel things to you on the beach that one day, about Shawn. All I can say is that I don't know why people die, and I don't know how to deal with it. I wish I could find some peace ease to all the pain in my life. My grandmother is sending me to a psychiatrist three days a week to work through some of these things, and she forbids me to go anywhere by myself.

Well, I didn't intend for this to be a sad story about my horrid life. I wanted to let you know I appreciated your support, and I'd like to keep in touch with you. I wish my life were like yours—innocent and free, with a real family on a Wisconsin farm. Sounds pretend.

Well, please say hi to Todd for me. You are so lucky to have him.

Yours,

Alissa

Christy cried over the letter more than once. Being so far away from Alissa, all she could do was write her back. But every letter she started, she ended up throwing away. She wanted to encourage Alissa somehow, give her some hope. But she couldn't find the right words. Everything sounded so phony.

Then there was the part about being so lucky to have Todd. That was a laugh! Christy didn't have Todd. Nobody had Todd. Things with him were as up and down as ever. They saw each other all the time at the beach, but when things started looking up, Tracy would appear and Christy would take the backseat again. Plus Todd had all his surfer friends, with whom Christy never managed to quite fit in. Some of them were pretty weird. A few too many conks on the head by a surfboard or something.

That very morning one of the guys had said, "Totally wasted!" when he came up from the water. He shook his head full of blond, curly hair so that the spray fell all over Christy.

"Thrashin', man! I was like, totally eating blue chunks." Then he stuck his board under his arm, mumbled, "Trash this," and walked away.

Christy had turned to Tracy. "Was I having a conversation with him? I think I need an interpreter."

"The waves aren't any good. He's going home," Tracy said.

"Oh. I'm glad Todd doesn't talk like that," Christy said, looking out at the water, watching Todd skim the waves on his familiar orange surfboard.

"Todd kind of talks everybody's language. He has his surfer friends, but then he hangs out with all the straight kids, too."

"You know him pretty well, don't you?" Christy ventured.

"I guess."

It seemed strange to Christy that Tracy was always friendly. Christy had to work hard at maintaining her coolness toward Tracy because she was such a free spirit and so likable. Why didn't Tracy fight harder for Todd's attention?

Finally, Christy came right out and asked her, "Tracy, do you like Todd?"

"Todd? I love Todd."

"Then why don't you get jealous when he does things with other girls?" For good measure, Christy threw in, "Like tomorrow, for instance, he's taking me to Disneyland for my birthday."

"Oh, really?" Tracy remarked without a hint of envy. "I hope you have fun! Happy birthday, too, if I don't see you tomorrow."

"Thanks," muttered Christy, not content to let her question go unanswered. "Doesn't that bother you or anything?"

"No, not a bit. Todd and I have been friends since last summer. The same guy led us both to the Lord here on the beach."

"What do you mean he 'led' you to the Lord?"

"I mean, he told us how to become Christians."

"You mean how you're supposed to ask forgiveness for your

sins and ask Christ to come into your heart?" Christy asked.

"Exactly. Have you done that, too?"

"No, I haven't done that exactly, but I'm still a Christian," Christy said.

"Well, I know this could sound harsh," Tracy said, "but nobody can become a Christian by just being good. That's why Christ died on—"

"I know all that!" Christy cut her off. "I don't know why everyone has to talk about sin so much."

"Because that's what separates us from God. As long as we're separated from Him, we'll never be able to become the people He wants us to be."

"I don't know what you mean."

"Haven't you ever felt guilty for stuff and wished you could unload it all and start fresh?"

Christy flashed back over the past week and all the guilt she felt over her behavior toward her aunt. "Yes. Of course." Then she thought of Alissa's letter.

"You don't have to live with that. You can be free from all that junk if you ask forgiveness from God and ask Jesus to come into your life and be your Lord."

Christy felt uncomfortable. She envied Tracy's openness and the way she talked about God as though He were a close friend, not a distant, almighty power ready to strike whenever someone did something He didn't like.

"You make it sound as though you and God are friends," Christy said, beginning to let down her guard.

"We are. Best friends."

"I don't know. I always thought God was way up there, and I was way down here, and it was up to me to be a good person."

While they talked, Todd came in from surfing. Playfully

shaking himself like a wet dog, he sprayed water all over the girls, who squealed and laughed.

"Watch it! You're dripping on my legs!" Christy protested. "It'll leave those salt dots."

"Salt dots, huh? There's only one way to get rid of salt dots." Todd got a mischievous gleam in his eye.

Christy shot a glance at Tracy, who nodded a quick yes to Todd. Before Christy realized what was happening, Todd grabbed her by both wrists, pulled her up, and started dragging her toward the water.

"No, no!" she screamed. "I'll go in by myself."

As soon as Todd let go of her wrists, she ran in the other direction, laughing and looking behind to see if Todd was chasing her. Doug saw all the action and blocked Christy's escape, grabbing her arm.

"Hold her!" Todd yelled.

Christy squealed, "No, no! Let me go!"

"Ready for a dip?" Todd asked, taking hold of her ankles.

"No! Stop, you guys!" Christy struggled, but with Doug holding her wrists and Todd holding her ankles, she couldn't wiggle free. They lifted her and trotted down to the water's edge.

"On three," Todd commanded as they swung her over the foamy waves. "One, two, three!"

They let go, and Christy landed in about four feet of water with a mighty splash. Completely drenched, she rose to her feet and shouted, "I'm going to get you guys back! Just wait!"

Doug had jogged up to the dry sand. Todd remained at the shoreline.

"What's that?" Todd said. "You want to go bodysurfing?" He high-stepped through the water to where Christy stood with her hands on her hips.

"Come on," he shouted. "Dive under."

Together they plunged beneath the oncoming wave. They swam out to where the waves were building, and for more than an hour, they rode the surging water together.

Don't let this day ever end, Christy thought as another wave lifted her, carried her, and exhilarated her. *Please don't let this feeling go away. Ever!*

As Christy lay on her bed later, with Alissa's letter still in her hand and the light fading in the room, she could feel the churning force of the ocean once more. And the exhilaration of not only riding the waves, but also of being with Todd. That was today. Who knew what tomorrow would be like with on-again-off-again Todd? Tomorrow. A day at Disneyland. With Todd. Would it be awful, like the concert, or wonderful, like the bodysurfing? Her thoughts were interrupted by a knock at the door.

"Christy?" came Uncle Bob's voice. "Telephone, hon. It's your mom and dad."

"Thanks, Uncle Bob," she said as he handed her the cordless phone. It was a typical conversation with her parents. Her mom tried to slowly bring the topic around to the point she wanted to make, but her dad cut in and jabbed the sharp words at Christy: "You need to come home Sunday."

"Sunday!" she squawked. "You mean this Sunday?"

"Yes, this Sunday."

"That's only three days away! I'm supposed to stay here till the end of August!"

"Don't make this any harder than it already is," he barked gruffly. "Your vacation is over. Now. Don't miss your plane."

"But, Dad—" she began, but then she heard the click on the other end, indicating that he had hung up.

Her mom was still on the line, though. "I gave Bob all the flight information, honey. He said you've been having a wonderful time."

"Mom, why do I have to come home?" Christy fought the tears with all her might.

"You just do, Christy. We'll explain everything when you get here Sunday."

Christy hung up the phone and slid under the covers on her bed, feeling cold all of a sudden. She wanted to cry, but the tears didn't come. Everything seemed so pointless. She had to go home in three days, and she didn't know why. Was it her dad's farm? Were things going worse for them financially? Or was she the problem? Were her parents punishing her for something? What had she done? She had kept her promise; she hadn't done anything she regretted. At least not yet. But she still had three more days, starting with her birthday tomorrow with Todd. Her birthday. Neither of her parents had even said, "Happy birthday." With that sharp realization came the tears. Bitter, salty, angry tears.

CHAPTER THIRTEEN

The Magic Kingdom

Todd showed up right at 9:00 the next morning. Christy fumbled for her sandals.

"I can't believe he's on time!" she said in a panic to her aunt.

"I'll go chat with him," Marti offered. "Hurry along."

Christy took one last look in the closet mirror. She loved this outfit. The denim shorts and peach-colored T-shirt were some of the new clothes from Aunt Marti, but she'd tried them on together only two days ago and decided they were the most comfortable of all her new clothes. If she was going to be shipwrecked on a tropical island, this is the outfit she'd want to be wearing.

Disneyland may not exactly be the same as a tropical adventure, but Christy felt as if she were going into parts unknown. She would never again have this kind of freedom. When she returned to Wisconsin, she knew her parents would clamp down on everything—makeup, dating, clothes, curfews. She had better enjoy it all now, while she had the chance.

She took the stairs lightly and greeted Todd with a confident "Hi!" Todd looked like his usual casual self in his shorts and white T-shirt.

"You two have a marvelous time!" Aunt Marti grinned approvingly.

"When do you think you'll be home?" Bob asked.

"When do you want Christy back, sir?" Todd asked.

"Make a day of it, kids," Bob said, waving his hand in the air. "We won't be worried unless it's midnight, and we haven't heard from you."

"Bye," they both called out and walked toward Gus. Christy thought she was going to burst with excitement and anticipation. Then Todd opened the front door of the van, and there sat Tracy, like a rock.

"Hi!" Tracy greeted her. "Happy birthday!"

Christy lost it right then and there. "Is this your idea of a surprise present?" she snarled at Todd. "I didn't think anybody else was going to Disneyland with us."

"I'm just dropping her off at work," Todd said calmly.

"Oh. I'm sorry," Christy whispered, completely ashamed.

"That's okay," Tracy said reluctantly, then handed her a box. "Here. This is for you. Happy birthday."

Todd drove to Hanson's Parlor in silence.

Christy felt awful. *Why did I have to go and ruin the whole day like that?*

"You can open it whenever you want," Tracy said, jumping out of the van. "I'm sorry I upset you. I wasn't trying to."

"I know, Tracy," Christy said, moving up to the front passenger seat. "I was just being a jerk. I'm sorry."

"Don't worry about it." Tracy's bounce returned. "I hope you guys have a really fun time! Think of me as I slave over gallons of ice cream all day."

They drove in silence for a few miles before Christy looked over at Todd. His teeth were clenched, which made his jaw look even more solid and manly.

"You okay?" she asked quietly.

"Not really."

"Is it because of how I acted with Tracy?"

"No, that's something between the two of you. Tracy doesn't have a problem with me spending the day with you. I'm not sure why you have a problem with me taking her to work."

"I don't. I guess I'm jealous of her in some ways."

"There's no reason to be. She's about the most loving, caring person you'll ever meet."

She looked at Tracy's gift, which she still held in her lap. "I wonder if I should open this now."

"Sure. Go ahead. I already know what it is. I hope you like it."

Christy read the card written in Tracy's handwriting:

For Christy,
We hope this will help you understand everything we've been saying about the Lord. Happy Birthday!

> *Love,*
> *Tracy and Todd*

"This is from you, too?" Christy asked Todd, tearing off the paper.

"Yeah. I picked it out, but Tracy made the cover and wrapped it and everything."

Christy pulled back the paper and lifted up a Bible. The cover was made from pink quilted fabric with tiny white flowers around the edges. Two white satin ribbons were attached as book markers.

"This is really nice, Todd. Thanks!" She secretly wished it had been something more personal. A Bible was something she imagined her Sunday school teacher giving her.

"Glad you like it," he said, his smile returning. He stuck a Debbie Stevens tape in the tape deck, rolled down the window, and cranked up the volume.

Christy rolled her window down, too, welcoming the breeze. She wanted to start this day all over and concentrate on the time she had with Todd. She wasn't going to let today slip through her fingers the way their bike ride to Balboa Island had.

"Did I tell you I went surfing this morning?" Todd asked.

"This morning? You're kidding! When?"

"About 6:30. My dad woke me up when he left for work."

"Were the waves any good?"

"Naw. Just ankle slappers. I hung out on my board for a while, but this whole thing with Shawn is really tearing me up. We used to get up early and go surfing."

"Really? I never would have guessed. You guys are so different. Or, I mean were so different. Or whatever you're supposed to say."

"It's okay; I know what you mean."

They chatted easily, and within a short time, Todd pulled Gus into the Disneyland parking lot entrance and handed the parking lot attendant a $50 bill for the parking.

"Do you have anything smaller?" the attendant asked.

"Let me check."

Christy watched as Todd peeled through a huge wad of bills until he came to a bunch of twenties.

Where did he get all the money? Christy wondered. *Maybe Disneyland is more expensive than I realized.*

"Well, you ready for the Magic Kingdom?" Todd asked, locking up Gus.

Christy smiled.

"Good," he said, stuffing his keys into his pocket. "I think it's ready for you."

Todd paid for their all-day passes at the front gate, and as they entered, Christy pointed to the flower garden that formed a picture of Mickey Mouse. "When I was little, I saw that on TV, and

I tried to get my mom to plant our flowers to look like that!"

Todd laughed. "Did she?"

"No. I tried to do it myself with rocks and dirt clods, though. Didn't turn out very well. I wish I had a camera with me. I'd take a picture of it."

"I don't think so, Christy," Todd said, shaking his head and grinning. "You don't take a camera to Disneyland. Makes you look like those people over there—tourists."

Todd pointed to a family on Main Street. The large mother and three pudgy kids were standing in front of a barber shop quartet, which was riding a bicycle built for four. The family members nearly hid the quartet. The father was bending backward in a hilarious position, apparently trying to get it all in his viewfinder. Todd and Christy looked at each other and muffled their laughter.

"Must be from the Midwest," Todd teased.

"Hey!" Christy socked him in the arm. "Watch it. I'm from the Midwest."

Todd shot her a sideways glance, his dimples showing as he suppressed a laugh. "I know."

Then he held out his hand for Christy to take. "Come on. Let's get on some rides."

Christy slid her hand into his and felt a warm rush spread through her fingers, up her arm, and through her whole body. *Don't let go!* she thought. *Don't ever, ever let go!*

They waited in line for half an hour to go on the bobsleds. Todd said this was his favorite ride and they had to go on this one first. They talked and laughed and even struck up a conversation with the people in line behind them.

Todd stepped into the shiny red bobsled first and slid all the way back, his legs pressed against the sides.

"Step in, please," the ride attendant directed. He was dressed in green knickers and kneesocks. He looked like a goatherd.

"Where do I sit?" Christy asked.

"Here." Todd patted the slice of seat right in front of him.

For a moment Christy thought she would never fit there. Then the attendant took her elbow and hurried her. She stepped in cautiously and wedged her body in.

"Am I squishing you?" she asked.

Suddenly, the bobsled lurched forward and began its steep climb to the top of the Matterhorn.

"Relax," Todd said. "It's okay. You look like you're about to jump out."

"I'm thinking about it," Christy admitted, cautiously leaning against Todd's chest. He felt solid and warm and oh, how she wished he would wrap his arms around her!

The clinking sound of the rails beneath them slowed to almost a stop at the crest of the Matterhorn. Christy looked straight ahead, and all she saw was sky. Fear gripped her. She grabbed the handrails inside the bobsled, squeezed her eyes shut, and let out a wild shriek of sheer terror as the sled plummeted down the other side of the mountain. Forget snuggling! Forget the tender moment! Hanging on was all that counted.

Several sharp turns and dips later, the racing bobsled splashed through the water and jerked to a stop. Another attendant offered his hand to help her out.

"You okay?" Todd asked, directing her to the exit.

"Yes." Her whole body trembled, and she felt silly for screaming.

"That was just our appetizer ride. Now I think you're ready for Space Mountain." Todd had a look of boyish excitement in his eyes.

"How about something to drink first? I think I need a few minutes to recover."

All day long they went on rides and ate and went on rides. After buying something to eat from every snack cart and experiencing every attraction in Tomorrowland, they headed for Adventureland.

Climbing atop the Swiss Family Robinson tree house, they looked out over the amusement park. Todd talked about his dream to someday live on a tropical island.

"I'm going to surf all day, eat papayas and mangos, and sip coconut juice right from the coconut."

"Sounds exotic," Christy said. "Are you going to live in a tree house like this one?"

"Yup. I'm going to sleep in a hammock, too."

"And what are you going to do for money?"

"Oh, I'll just trade beads with the natives and live off the land."

"You know, you would have made a great hippie."

"I probably would have. My dad always says he was the last hippie."

"You're kidding."

"Nope. He met my mom at Berkeley during a protest march, and they moved in together the next morning—after they got out of jail, that is."

"I don't believe it," Christy scoffed.

"It's true!"

After the tree house, they waited in line for almost an hour for the Pirates of the Caribbean ride. When they got off, they decided to wait in line to eat dinner at the Blue Bayou Restaurant. About half an hour later, they were seated. Neither of them was very hungry, but they were glad for a cool, quiet place to sit. Their table was only a few feet from where the Pirates of the Caribbean boats launched for their journey. The fake, twinkling fireflies were what Christy liked best.

"Isn't this relaxing? I feel like I've been transported to another time and place. I can't believe how real these little fireflies look. They are pretend, aren't they?"

"Of course," Todd said with a laugh. "Amazing how real they can make stuff look now, huh? Do you know what you want yet?"

The panic that usually seized her at a time like this didn't appear. "The chicken sounds good. Although, to be honest, I'm not real hungry."

They took their time eating, and when the waiter brought the check, Todd laid down a $50 bill. Christy thought back over the day. Todd had tossed around cash like it was play money. He had paid for everything, including a sweatshirt and a little Winnie the Pooh stuffed toy.

Todd crammed the change into his pocket and asked, "Well, what do you want to do now?"

"Let's go on some more rides. And then I need to find a souvenir for my little brother back home."

Todd took her hand as they left the Blue Bayou and held it as they strolled through New Orleans Square. Oh, how she wished her hands weren't so sweaty! Would Todd notice? His hand felt so strong and sure. She loved feeling close to him and secure as they slid through the crowds.

"Hey, how 'bout one of those for your brother?" Todd pointed to a mound of Mickey Mouse hats in a shop window. They darted in, laughing at each other as they tried on all the different hats. Finally, they agreed on a black pirate's hat with a long blue feather.

"David will love this! I just hope I can get it home in decent shape."

"When are you going back?" Todd asked as they got in line for the Jungle Cruise.

"That's something I wanted to tell you." Christy held his

hand a little tighter. "My parents called last night and told me I had to come home right away. I'm leaving Sunday."

"This Sunday? The day after tomorrow?"

"Yes."

"Why?" Todd asked. Christy thought she could read a look of disappointment on his face. "School doesn't start for five more weeks. I don't even leave for my mom's until the first of September."

"I know, but I guess things aren't going so great, and my parents want me home so we can go through it together."

"Go through what?"

"Well, the only thing I can figure out is that it must be the farm. I think I told you that my dad's a farmer. Not as exciting as a reformed hippie, I know. But we haven't really made it financially for the past three or four years, and my dad has sold off a lot of our land. I guess a bunch of stuff has happened since I left. I'm not sure what's going on. All I know is that they want me home right away."

"That's really too bad," Todd said, giving her hand a squeeze.

"I'm going to miss you, Todd. We'll have to write or something."

"I'm not much of a writer, to be honest."

"Well, Tallahassee's not as far away from Wisconsin as California is. Is it?"

Todd laughed at her logic. "I don't know."

They had made it to the front of the line and stepped down into the boat. The ride operator, dressed in safari gear, advised the passengers to keep their hands and arms inside the moving vehicle at all times, warning them of the untamed animals they would encounter ahead.

Todd slipped his arm around the back of the seat. "This used to be my favorite ride when I was a kid."

"I thought the bobsleds were."

"Well, okay, this one and the bobsleds."

He looked like a kid now, eagerly taking in all the fake jungle bird sounds. She could almost imagine him swinging on one of those jungle vines. *You Tarzan, me Jane*. Her mind drifted, creating a jungle romance.

"Just ahead," the driver spoke into his microphone, "are the wild hippos. But have no fear, folks. They're only dangerous when they wiggle their ears!"

Christy looked over her shoulder at the wild hippos rising out of the water, only a few feet away from her. The largest one opened its jaws and, to her surprise, began to wiggle its ears.

"Oh, no, folks! Look out! He's wiggling his ears!" The driver grabbed his cap gun and shot rapidly at the beast.

Completely startled, Christy let out a scream and threw herself onto Todd's chest. The elderly couple next to them started laughing, and their small grandson patted Christy on the leg, saying, "Don't cry, lady. Monster all gone!"

Everyone on the boat watched as Christy peeled herself off of an embarrassed Todd. The driver made the most of the situation.

"It's okay, folks, the young lady will be all right. Actually, we hired her to come along and add some excitement to Disneyland's own version of the Love Boat."

Everyone laughed. Christy was totally embarrassed, but she laughed, too. Todd slipped his arm around her and smiled an easy smile that said a thousand things to Christy. She read something deep and wonderful in his silver-blue eyes—or did she?

That's when Christy began to wonder if he would kiss her good night when they got home. It flooded her thoughts so she barely paid attention to what they did the rest of the night. She didn't listen to what Todd said. Instead, she drew inward, self-conscious about how she looked, wondering if she would bump into his nose when they kissed, how she should hold her mouth . . . It was torture!

Around 9:00, they stopped outside of Bear Country and watched the nightly fireworks display. Todd put his arm around her, and she rested her head on his shoulder, feeling the same bright explosions inside as each fireworks burst in the night sky. In the distance, they watched as a real live Tinkerbell, hooked on a cable, "flew" from the top of the Matterhorn, across the Magic Kingdom to Fantasyland.

As they were leaving the park, they made one last stop at the Emporium and watched the glassblower make a tiny Tinkerbell figurine. The liquid-hot glass looked like clear bubble gum as the craftsman pulled and pinched and twisted it about his blue-flamed blowtorch.

"That's so amazing," Christy said when the craftsman had finished and held up the figurine.

"You want it?" Todd asked.

"Well, I don't know." Christy hesitated. Every time she had looked at something twice or said she liked it, Todd had pulled out his bank roll and bought it for her.

"Excuse me," Todd said to the salesclerk in a long dress and white pinafore. "Could we get that glass Tinkerbell he just made?"

"Certainly," she said and gently wrapped the tiny fairy in tissue paper and placed it in a box.

"Thanks, Todd." Christy squeezed his arm. "I really appreciate your getting me all these things. Thanks."

"It's all right," Todd said casually. "Want anything else to eat?"

"Are you kidding? I don't think I can eat another bite for a week!"

They walked out on Main Street, and Christy noticed all the

little white twinkling lights strung on the trees. *It really is a fairy-tale land*, she thought.

Juggling all her shopping bags, she realized Todd had his hands full of bags, too. She hadn't remembered buying this much, but now the bags felt heavy and burdensome. Her feet ached, her throat ached, her arms ached. If she went on one more ride, she would be too tired to scream.

"Anything else you want to see?" Todd asked.

"Just a nice place to sit down."

"How about Gus?"

"Sounds good."

They rode the shuttle through the parking lot, balancing all the bags on their laps. Most of the cars had disappeared from the lot that was several times bigger than her hometown park.

It was a mellow ride home in Gus, both of them too tired to say much. Christy probably would have fallen asleep except her mind kept torturing her about the moment when their date would end. She played the scene over and over in her imagination. Would he kiss her? What would it be like? Should she close her eyes? What if she had bad breath? She could hardly stand the suspense.

Finally, the moment arrived when Todd walked her to the front door. It was almost midnight. Her heart pounded wildly. She swallowed hard.

"Thanks, Todd. This was the best birthday I ever, ever had." She looked up at him shyly, expectantly.

He put his arms around her and hugged her tightly. "Good night, Christy," he said softly. And then he pulled away without kissing her.

"Good night," Christy echoed, hiding her disappointment.

Todd stuck his hands into his pockets and headed toward Gus.

Then, as if he had forgotten something, he turned around. Christy's heart froze.

He's coming back! Now what should I do? Is he going to kiss me now?

"I almost forgot," Todd said with a laugh. "Here." He pulled a wad of money from his pocket and handed it to Christy.

"What's this for?"

"Your aunt. It's what's left over."

"What do you mean? I don't get it."

"It's left over from the money your aunt gave me to take you to Disneyland. We didn't spend it all, so I thought you should give her the rest back."

The blood drained from Christy's face. "You mean my aunt asked you to take me today, and she even gave you the money!"

"Hey! It's cool. We had a great time. I'm glad she talked me into it."

"Talked you into it!"

Christy turned on her heels and jerked the front door open, catapulting up the stairs. In her fury, she stumbled on the third step and lost her sandal. With the rage of a wild warrior, she grabbed her sandal, heaved it toward Todd and fled to her room. Some day in the Magic Kingdom! So much for happily ever after! Her "fairy godmother" was only her aggravating aunt, and her handsome prince had just turned into a toad!

CHAPTER FOURTEEN

The Promise

The digital clock on the nightstand read "12:04." The sun shining in through Christy's bedroom window was so bright, it seemed to shout at her. She didn't feel much better than she had 12 hours earlier when she had thrown her shoe at Todd, flung the money in her aunt's face, and screamed, "Get out of my life!" As a grand finale, she had heaved a pillow at her uncle when he followed her into her room to try to talk to her.

They were wise to let her sleep, to leave her alone for the last 12 hours. Christy knew she couldn't burrow in her bed any longer; she had to rise and face the inevitable. Things needed to be settled with her aunt, and she had to pack before her plane left tomorrow morning.

Thinking about all those hard issues only pressed her deeper into her pillow. She felt gunky. Her top eyelashes stuck to the bottom lashes, her teeth seemed encased in caramel corn, her eyes were puffy from crying, and she was all tangled up in her Disneyland clothes.

Strewn across the floor were the shopping bags she had thrown hither and yon in her fury. Bags filled with all the souvenirs Todd had bought for her. Or rather, her aunt had financed

Todd to get for her. Her room was a mess, she was a mess, her life was a mess.

"That's the problem with hissy fits," Paula had said once. "You always have to clean up after yourself, and it's very humbling."

What humbled Christy at that moment was seeing her new Bible fanned out on the floor where it had landed after being ejected from a flying bag. Meekly, she slithered out of bed and retrieved it, smoothing down the wrinkled pages.

"I'm sorry," she whispered. "It's just that I don't think any of this is fair. Why did my aunt make such a fool out of me? Why did Todd go along with her? And why do I have to go home tomorrow? Now things will never work out between Todd and me!"

Christy realized she was talking to God as if it were the most natural thing for her to do, just like her new friends talked to Him. "I don't know what my problem is," she continued. "I just feel like I'm losing it. Like everything around me is going under. What am I doing wrong, God?"

In the silence that followed, a piercing thought came to Christy—the nightmare she had had weeks ago. The memory so filled her mind that the feelings all came back, rushing toward her with urgent freshness. It was as if she were, once again, barely hanging on to the side of the boat. The tentacles of seaweed were wrapping themselves tighter and tighter around her legs. She was facing that terrifying moment all over again, the moment when she had to decide whether to get into the boat or let the seaweed pull her under. Only this time she was wide awake, and the dream paralleled reality too strongly for her to ignore it. Jesus was that boat, like Todd had said. And if she ever wanted to get to heaven (or Hawaii, as Todd had called it), she had to get in the boat.

She knew what she had to do, and she knew she had to do it now. Christy knelt beside her bed, bowed her head, and closed her eyes. Then she spoke aloud in a soft voice.

"God, I realize that what's missing in my life is You. I mean, I've known about You my whole life, but I don't know You the same way Todd or Tracy do. And I want to know You personally, like they said. I really want You to come into my life. So, Lord, please forgive all my sins and come into my life right now. I promise my whole heart to You forever. Amen."

She opened her eyes and turned to study her reflection in the mirror. She looked the same as when she had pulled herself out of bed—hair a mess, clothes wrinkled, raccoon eyes from smeared mascara. But inside she knew she was different. Not wildly emotional or anything, just clean. Secure. Happy. She smiled and hugged her Bible close to her. She was in the boat, and the adventure was just beginning.

The first big wave ahead would be facing Aunt Marti.

Christy showered and dressed quickly. She found her aunt and uncle sitting on the patio, sipping iced tea. Quietly, Christy slid past her aunt and settled on the chaise lounge next to her uncle's chair. They both acted as though she weren't there, waiting for her to make the first move.

"About last night . . . ," Christy began, rubbing her hands together, "I think I owe you an apology."

"No, darling." Aunt Marti turned to face her. "I realize that it is I who owes you an apology."

Uncle Bob remained quiet with a furrowed brow, as if he were unsure where this conversation would lead.

"I was terribly at fault, and I'm not sure I can ever forgive myself for not preparing you for your first experience."

"Well . . . ," Christy fumbled, "it's not that you didn't . . . I mean, I really shouldn't have expected anything more, I guess. It's just that I really thought Todd wanted to be with me, just because he liked me, but . . ."

"No, Christy, don't blame yourself. And don't blame Todd. It's my fault. I really should have seen it coming and done more to prepare you."

"It just hurts, that's all. And I felt so stupid. So used."

"Yes," Aunt Marti agreed, "men can make you feel that way—especially the first time."

"What do you mean, 'Men can make you feel that way'?" Christy asked belligerently. "You made me feel that way, Aunt Martha!"

"*I* made you feel that way! How could I possibly make you feel used?"

"By giving Todd all that money and bribing him into taking me to Disneyland!"

Aunt Marti stared at her in disbelief. "You mean, that's what all the tears were about last night? The screaming and the turmoil were simply over my helping to finance your birthday excursion?"

"Yes." Christy stared back. "What did you think I was so upset about?"

Bob interjected: "You don't want to know what she thinks you were upset about. She's lost all comprehension of youthful innocence. Too many soap operas. It's warped her mind."

"It has not, Robert! I resent you saying such a thing! Here I was, honestly concerned that Christy had her first intimate encounter with a young man and feeling guilty for not doing more to prepare her!"

Christy was stunned. She had been worried about whether or not Todd would kiss her, and her aunt was imagining much more.

"Why, I have done nothing but lavish my love on you all summer long," her aunt continued. "I've given you everything a young girl could dream of. Your uncle and I have made a great number of sacrifices for you, and if this is all the thanks we get, then, perhaps it's for the best that you're leaving tomorrow. Maybe once you're gone, you'll appreciate all we've bought for you."

Christy wanted to rush over to her aunt, first to hug her and then slug her. How could she think in such a twisted way? How could she take a situation and bend it so that Christy came out the guilty party? Yet, she was right, too. Christy had taken all the clothes and dinners out and excursions for granted.

"Aunt Marti," Christy began cautiously, hoping to melt her aunt's frosty stare, "it's just that there are some things you can't buy with money."

As soon as she said it, Christy thought of the Debbie Stevens song "You Won't Find It at the Mall." Now she really knew what that song meant.

"But," she added quickly, "I appreciate all that you have done for me. I really do. I'll never forget this summer. It's been the best summer of my whole life!"

Aunt Marti didn't respond. She stared out at the ocean, her lips pulled tight with anger. "I have nothing more to say, Christina."

"I'm sorry," Christy said with tears in her eyes. "I'm sorry for being such a problem to both of you."

"You know we loved having you here." Uncle Bob reached over and gave Christy's shoulder a squeeze. "Why don't you enjoy your last afternoon and go join your friends down on the beach?"

"I don't know if I ever want to see Todd again. Or what I'd say if I did."

"Sure you do. Besides, this is your last chance. Make the most of it, honey. And by the way, would this, by any chance, be yours?" He held up the sandal she had hurled at Todd.

"Yes," she said sheepishly and took it from him.

"Go ahead," Aunt Marti obliged. "You need to make up with Todd before you go home."

"I need to make up with you, too," Christy gently pointed out.

"All is forgiven," Aunt Marti said with a little smile.

Christy rushed over to her aunt and bent down to hug her. Laughing uncomfortably, as though she wasn't used to such affectionate displays, her aunt returned the hug.

"Now get going," she said, releasing Christy and smoothing her own slightly rumpled hair.

Twenty minutes later, Christy shuffled through the sand, wondering whom she would find down by the jetty. Alissa was back in Boston. Tracy was probably at work. Todd . . . who knew what Todd was doing.

After all, nobody paid Todd to spend time with me this afternoon, so why would he be hanging around?

She scanned the surfboards out in the water, but Todd's orange board wasn't among them. She approached the group that Todd tended to hang around with, but the only ones she knew were Heather, Doug, and Leslie. Remembering how she had felt like an outcast the night of the concert, Christy hesitated, not sure she wanted to face the group. But it was too late. They had already seen her and were motioning for her to join them.

"Hey, Christy," Doug greeted her, "you just missed Todd. He was here all morning. Said you guys had an awesome time at Disneyland!"

"Awesome?" teased Leslie. "Nobody uses that word anymore."

"Doug does!" Heather said with a giggle. "Tracy said she and Todd gave you a Bible. That was so cool of them."

"Oh, 'cool,' " Doug teased. "Now that's a real groovy word."

Heather wadded up a T-shirt and threw it at him.

"Yes," Christy said, trying to appear relaxed. "It's a really nice Bible." She wanted to tell them of her decision that morning to give her life to Jesus, but she didn't know how.

"We're all going to have a barbecue here tonight," Doug announced to her. "You should come."

"Where's it going to be?"

"Over there at the fire pits." Heather pointed. "Everybody just brings food, and we sit around and talk and sing and stuff. It's kind of our church group, but we try not to be cliquey. Michelle, Doug, and I are coming, and Todd said he might come and bring his guitar."

"Todd plays a guitar?" Christy asked.

"You didn't know that? He's really good."

For the next couple of hours, Christy talked to Heather while Doug rode his body board. She lay on her back the whole time to get as much sun on her face as possible, so that when she got off the plane the next day, everyone would know she had been to California.

Around 5:00, Christy headed back to the house to get some hot dogs for the barbecue and to grab her new Disneyland sweatshirt.

On the side table by the front door was a letter for her. She thought it was Paula's writing at first but then realized it was Alissa's. Come to think of it, Paula hadn't written her in a long time. Oh, well. Tomorrow she would be home and could tell Paula all about Disneyland, the catastrophe with Todd, and opening her heart to the Lord. So much had happened in such a short time.

Christy sat on the bottom step and skimmed the letter from Alissa. She sounded a little better than she had in her last letter, but maybe that was because of the new boyfriend she mentioned. Her grandmother even approved of him. A college sophomore named Everett, but everyone called him Bret. She sounded pretty happy with him, but Christy wondered how long that would last.

Christy stuck the letter back in the envelope and decided she would write Alissa on the plane. She felt she now had some answers to offer. Having Jesus in her heart made her feel as though she weren't all alone anymore, trying to figure things out on her own. *Alissa needs that kind of friend*, Christy thought. *Somebody who isn't going to leave her.*

Christy pushed her bedroom door open and found Uncle Bob folding a pair of her jeans into a suitcase.

"I hope you don't mind," he said. "I think we'll need to get a few boxes or another suitcase. Seems you're going home with more than you brought!"

"You don't have to do that. I can do it later."

"Well, your aunt's made reservations for 6:30 at the Five Crowns Restaurant, so I thought I'd get a head start for you."

"Oh, no!" Christy moaned. "I was going to go cook hot dogs on the beach with everybody. We don't have to go out to eat, do we?"

"I think she wanted to make your last night here special."

"It will be special if I can spend it with my friends," Christy pleaded.

"Well," he said, his eyes twinkling, "tell you what. You go have your cookout with your friends. Don't worry about your aunt. I'll take care of her."

"You are so awesome!" Christy threw her arms around his neck and hugged him.

"Awesome?" he repeated. "Is that good?"

"Definitely!"

Christy spent a few minutes in front of the mirror, fixing her hair. Then she splashed her face with cool water and smoothed some Aloe gel over her sunburned cheeks. She looked like a true California girl: dark tan, sun-streaked hair.

I'm going to move to California as soon as I'm old enough, she decided. *Maybe I'll go to college out here*. This was her real home now. She felt no connection with cows and snowdrifts and all that went with Wisconsin living. Palm trees and surfboards—that was more her real self now.

Christy dabbed on some mascara, grabbed her sweatshirt, and slipped downstairs to the kitchen, where Bob, with a wink, handed her a bag of cookout food. Christy rushed to the fire ring, where some of the guys had already started a fire. Tracy stood there, straightening out coat hangers to cook the hot dogs on. Cute, petite Tracy with her quick smile and big brown eyes. Christy had tried so hard not to like her, but now she realized how much she was going to miss her.

"Christy! Todd told me you're going home tomorrow. I can't believe it!" She tossed the coat hangers down and gave Christy a friendly hug. "We're going to miss you so much."

Christy quickly looked around. Todd wasn't there. She was disappointed and relieved at the same time.

"Thanks," she said as she hugged Tracy back. "And thanks, too, for the Bible and the cover you made. I really like it."

"I'm so glad. After our little encounter yesterday morning, I wasn't sure if I should give it to you or not," Tracy said.

"Well, I'm glad you did. Do you know if Todd is going to come tonight?"

"I don't know. Hey, Brian, do you know if Todd's coming?"

"He was out here this morning when we were talking about it, but he didn't say."

"Who knows with Mr. Unpredictable," chimed in Michelle.

Well said, Christy thought.

For the next hour or so she kept looking, hoping that Todd would show up and yet wondering what she would say to him if he did—or what he would say to her. After awhile, she quit watching for him and tried to push him out of her mind. Everyone else was being so nice to her that it made it easy to have a fun time. Christy quietly thought about how much she was going to miss this new group of friends. She watched as the sun slipped into the ocean like a huge orange beach ball and wished she'd gotten to know all of them better. She also wished again that she didn't have to go home.

"So what if Todd isn't here with his guitar," Tracy said as the sky began to darken. "Let's sing anyway."

The group, 11 of them, gathered around the fire and began singing choruses that Christy had never heard before. Some of them were soft and gentle, others loud and spirited. But they were all about the Lord, or rather songs that they sang to the Lord. She recognized some of the songs as verses she'd learned in Sunday school.

This is the most beautiful place in the world, Christy thought. *What a perfect night! If only Todd were here. If only we hadn't ended last night in such an awful way. This clear night sky, these gentle breezes, and these songs are all so wonderful. I don't want to go home. I want to stay here forever!*

Michelle must have noticed Christy's tears glistening in the firelight, because she leaned over and said, "It's probably going to be really hard for you to go home."

Christy's cheeks stung from salty tears on her sunburn. "I don't want to go."

"It'll turn out all right. You'll see."

The next song they sang was another Bible verse.

Trust in the Lord
With all your heart
And lean not on
Your own understanding.
In all your ways acknowledge Him
And He will direct your paths.

Christy had never felt her heart so full. The group huddled around the fire until the last log snapped and fell into a mound of red-hot embers. Then they went around the circle, and everyone prayed. Some prayed for their families, some prayed for their friends—that they would become Christians. Others thanked God for things He had done for them. Christy was the second to the last one to pray. Surprisingly, the words came easily.

"Dear Lord, I want to thank You for coming into my life this morning. Please be with my family and the problems we're having now, and please be with me when I go home tomorrow. Amen."

The next person, Doug, didn't pray. Instead, he put his arm around Christy and pulled her close. "Did you really?" he asked.

"What?" Christy looked up, startled.

Everyone was looking at her.

"Did you really ask Christ into your heart this morning?"

"Yes," Christy answered, surprised at the reaction of everyone around her.

They all spoke at once: "That's great!" "Wow!" "You're kidding!" "I can't believe it!" "We've been praying for you!"

Everyone gathered around her in a big group hug, and Christy was amazed at how excited they all were. She never felt so loved and accepted. Doug gave her the biggest hug of all of them.

If only Todd had been there! It killed her, not knowing if she would ever see him again, especially after their closing scene at the door last night. She wasn't sure how they would have worked it out, but she was sure they could have, if they tried.

The group hung around the fire pit until everyone felt chilled from the night wind. About 11:00, Doug walked her home.

"So, did you have a good summer?" he asked, stroking his fingers through his short hair.

"It went too fast."

"I'm so glad I got to know you," he said. "You can't believe how excited I am that you became a Christian. You'll never be sorry."

"Does the Lord really help you when things are tough?" Christy asked.

"Of course. But you know He doesn't take away the rough times. He helps you through them. Besides, all the difficult stuff makes you grow. It helps you depend on Him and not on yourself."

They were at Bob and Marti's front steps, and Doug added. "At least that's what happens to me when I go through hard stuff."

"You know what I'm going to miss?" Christy asked, standing with her back to the front door. "I'm going to miss listening to people talk about God so easily and naturally. I've learned a lot from you guys this summer. I don't have any friends at home that love God the way you do."

"Well," Doug challenged, "you'll have to tell them. Start your own group of God-lovers."

"God-lovers?" she repeated.

"Or whatever you want to call them. It takes only one person."

Doug was so easy to talk to. Why didn't she like him the way she liked Todd? He was cute, nice, and caring, but there was just something about Todd.

Todd. Why wasn't Todd standing by the front door with me tonight instead of Doug? She knew she had ruined everything when she threw her shoe at him.

"I'd better go in," she told Doug, shivering a little in the damp air. "Good-bye! I hope I see you again sometime."

"Here," Doug said, giving her a big hug. "I'll see you in heaven, if not before."

Christy gave a little laugh and went inside. She found her

room completely cleaned and on the floor were three new leather suitcases, all packed but still open. A note from her uncle was pinned to her pillow: *Hope you had a good time. You'll need to get something out of your suitcase to wear tomorrow on the plane. I'll wake you up at 6:00 so you'll have time to get ready.*

Christy couldn't sleep. She had so much floating around in her mind. *Why didn't Todd show up tonight at the barbecue? Will I ever see him again? Why do I have to go home tomorrow? Why is life always so complicated?* She wore herself out trying to come up with the answers.

Finally, she released it all, thinking about Doug's statement that God would help her through the rough times instead of taking them away.

"Okay," Christy prayed, "I guess I'd better depend on You to help me through all these frustrating things, because I'm going to go crazy trying to figure them all out."

She snuggled under the warm covers, and then she softly sang, "Trust in the Lord with all your heart . . ."

She fell asleep before she finished.

The next morning Uncle Bob tapped on her door at 6:02. "We need to leave in an hour for the airport, Christy. Let me know if you need help with anything."

She showered and dressed in a daze. Her ears buzzed as if a toy airplane were circling round and round in her head. After curling her hair, she crammed the last bag of cosmetics into the last suitcase. Opening her door, she hollered, "I'm ready!"

Aunt Marti appeared in the hallway. "Are you sure you have everything, dear?"

Marti looked stunning in a bright yellow and navy blue outfit. Her cool composure reigned; nothing of their conflict from the day before remained. Apparently, Bob had smoothed over the restaurant situation, but Christy wisely thought she had better not bring it up.

"Yes, but I can't carry these suitcases. They're way too heavy."

Uncle Bob had to make a separate trip for each suitcase, throwing the leather monsters into the trunk. They pulled out of the driveway, and Christy tearfully took one last look at the house, one last gaze out at the beach, and allowed herself one last thought centered on Todd. It was all over. Her summer. Her first love . . .

The car stopped at a red light. This was the same intersection she and Todd had crossed on their bike ride. *Todd.* Just thinking about him caused a painful ache deep inside her. She swallowed the swelling wad of agony in her throat.

"Are my lights on?" Bob asked Marti.

"No."

"Then why is the guy in the car behind me flashing his lights and waving?"

Christy turned around. "It's Todd!" she screamed. "Don't go yet!"

"But, Christy darling, the light's turned green!" Marti protested.

Christy jumped out of the car and bounded toward Gus. Todd stepped out of the van, with the engine still running, and handed Christy a small bouquet of white carnations. Her favorite! How did he know? Had her aunt set him up again? At this point she didn't care.

"I'm glad you stopped!" Todd said with a smile that showed his dimples. "The horn's not working in ol' Gus this morning."

"Thanks for the flowers."

"That's okay. Hey, Tracy called me last night after she left the beach and told me about your decision to turn your life over to the Lord."

"Yes," Christy said shyly. "It all made sense finally, and I knew it was time to get in the boat, like you told me."

"Christy," Todd said, tentatively reaching over and touching her shoulder. "You have no idea how happy I am for you. I've been so bummed out about Shawn. But knowing that you've become a Christian . . . " He began to choke up. "It's just the best thing that could've ever happened."

"I know," Christy whispered. She quickly searched Todd's bronzed face for one last time, desperately trying to remember everything about him—his strong jaw, those faint dimples when he smiled, his sun-washed blond hair, and those screaming silver-blue eyes, which were now staring deeply into her eyes.

The driver in the car behind Todd, exasperated from waiting, pulled out around them and laid on the horn as he sped through the yellow light.

"I guess I'd better let you go." Todd's mouth turned up in one of his wonderful, confident grins. "I wrote down my address in Florida. It's on a card inside the flowers. I'm not promising I'll write a lot, but if you want to write me, I promise I'll write back."

"Okay," she agreed. Forcing back the tears, she whispered, "Bye, Todd."

He leaned down, right in the middle of the street, in front of the whole world, and gently pressed his lips against hers. A brief, tender kiss. The kind that only comes from innocent love and whose memory lasts a lifetime.

"I'm going to miss you," he whispered.

"I'm going to miss you, too!"

Todd glanced up and changed his tone, "Light's green again. You'd better go."

"Bye!" she called, dashing to the car. "I'll write you, I promise!"

Uncle Bob sped through the intersection, leaving Gus the Bus behind at the red light.

It was blissfully quiet for a few minutes as Christy pressed her lips against the bouquet of carnations, reliving the memory of her first kiss.

"Well," Aunt Marti clucked. "Just for the record, I had nothing to do with that rendezvous."

"You didn't? Really?" Christy's voice floated light and dreamy. "How did he know carnations were my favorite? And white carnations, too?"

"Kismet," Uncle Bob stated.

"What's that?"

"Some things you just can't explain. You have to figure a higher source is orchestrating the whole program."

"There is!" Christy agreed. "And I know Him personally."

"Well, that's nice, Christy dear. That's a very sweet way to think of God." Aunt Marti pulled down the visor to check her lipstick in the mirror.

"It's more than that. I made a promise this summer. To the Lord. I promised to give Him my whole heart. Now I'm trusting Him to work out whatever He thinks is best for my life."

"That's fine, dear." Aunt Marti pursed her lips together. "But my advice would be, don't overdo this religious approach to life. You control your own destiny, really, and there's no use waiting on God when you're perfectly capable of taking care of things yourself."

"Your aunt's right," Uncle Bob concurred. "As I told you weeks ago, 'To thine own self be true.' "

Christy laughed quietly and brushed the carnations against her cheek. "Nobody can control their own destiny, and I tried being true to myself, but I started going under. I'd rather be true to the Lord. It's way more fun! Besides, I know for sure that I'm going to make it to Hawaii now."

Marti cast a sideways glance at Bob and whispered, "What do you suppose she means by that?"

Bob gave her a look that said, "Who knows."

Christy smiled, brushing the carnations back and forth underneath her nose, breathing in the spicy-sweet fragrance. Inside she glowed with an unspeakable joy as her summer in California rolled out like the tide, leaving treasures on the shore of her heart, changing her life forever.

Don't Miss These Captivating Stories in
THE CHRISTY MILLER SERIES

#1 • Summer Promise
Christy spends the summer at the beach with her wealthy aunt and uncle. Will she do something she'll later regret?

#2 • A Whisper and a Wish
Christy is convinced that dreams do come true when her family moves to California and the cutest guy in school shows an interest in her.

#3 • Yours Forever
Fifteen-year-old Christy does everything in her power to win Todd's attention.

#4 • Surprise Endings
Christy tries out for cheerleader, learns a classmate is out to get her, and schedules two dates for the same night.

#5 • Island Dreamer
It's an incredible tropical adventure when Christy celebrates her sixteenth birthday on Maui.

#6 • A Heart Full of Hope
A dazzling dream date, a wonderful job, a great car. And lots of freedom! Christy has it all. Or does she?

#7 • True Friends
Christy sets out with the ski club and discovers the group is thinking of doing something more than hitting the slopes.

#8 • Starry Night
Christy is torn between going to the Rose Bowl Parade with her friends or on a surprise vacation with her family.

#9 • Seventeen Wishes
Christy is off to summer camp—as a counselor for a cabin of wild fifth-grade girls.

#10 • A Time to Cherish
A surprise houseboat trip! Her senior year! Lots of friends! Life couldn't be better for Christy until . . .

#11 • Sweet Dreams
Christy's dreams become reality when Todd finally opens his heart to her. But her relationship with her best friend goes downhill fast when Katie starts dating Michael, and Christy has doubts about their relationship.

#12 • A Promise Is Forever
On a European trip with her friends, Christy finds it difficult to keep her mind off Todd. Will God bring them back together?

THE SIERRA JENSEN SERIES

If you've enjoyed reading about Christy Miller,
you'll love reading about Christy's friend Sierra Jensen.

#1 • Only You, Sierra
When her family moves to another state, Sierra dreads going to a new high school—until she meets Paul.

#2 • In Your Dreams
Just when events in Sierra's life start to look up—she even gets asked out on a date—Sierra runs into Paul.

#3 • Don't You Wish
Sierra is excited about visiting Christy Miller in California during Easter break. Unfortunately, her sister, Tawni, decides to go with her.

#4 • Close Your Eyes
Sierra experiences a sticky situation when Paul comes over for dinner and Randy shows up at the same time.

#5 • Without a Doubt
When handsome Drake reveals his interest in Sierra, life gets complicated.

#6 • With This Ring
Sierra couldn't be happier when she goes to Southern California to join Christy Miller and their friends for Doug and Tracy's wedding.

#7 • Open Your Heart
When Sierra's friend Christy Miller receives a scholarship from a university in Switzerland, she invites Sierra to go with her and Aunt Marti to visit the school.

#8 • Time Will Tell
After an exciting summer in Southern California and Switzerland, Sierra returns home to several unsettled relationships.

#9 • Now Picture This
When Sierra and Paul start corresponding, she imagines him as her boyfriend and soon begins neglecting her family and friends.

#10 • Hold on Tight
Sierra joins her brother and several friends on a road trip to Southern California to visit potential colleges.

FOCUS ON THE FAMILY®

LIKE THIS BOOK?

Then you'll love *Brio* magazine! Written especially for teen girls, it's packed each month with 32 pages on everything from fiction and faith to fashion, food . . . even guys! Best of all, it's all from a Christian perspective! But don't just take our word for it. Instead, see for yourself by requesting a complimentary copy.

Simply write Focus on the Family, Colorado Springs, CO 80995 (in Canada, write P.O. Box 9800, Stn. Terminal, Vancouver, B.C. V6B 4G3) and mention that you saw this offer in the back of this book. You may also call 1-800-232-6459 (in Canada, call 1-800-661-9800).

You may also visit our Web site (www.family.org) to learn more about the ministry or find out if there is a Focus on the Family office in your country.

Have you heard about our "Classic Collection"? It's packed with drama and outstanding stories like Louisa May Alcott's *Little Women*, which features the complete text—updated for easier reading—and fascinating facts about the author. Did you know that the Alcott's home was a stop on the Underground Railroad? It's true! And every "Classic" edition packs similar information.

Call Focus on the Family at the number above, or check out your local Christian bookstore.

Focus on the Family is an organization that is dedicated to helping you and your family establish lasting, loving relationships with each other and the Lord. It's why we exist! If we can assist you or your family in any way, please feel free to contact us. We'd love to hear from you!